THE SILENT SACRIFICE

THE IMMORTAL TALE OF BARBARIK

RUDRA IYER

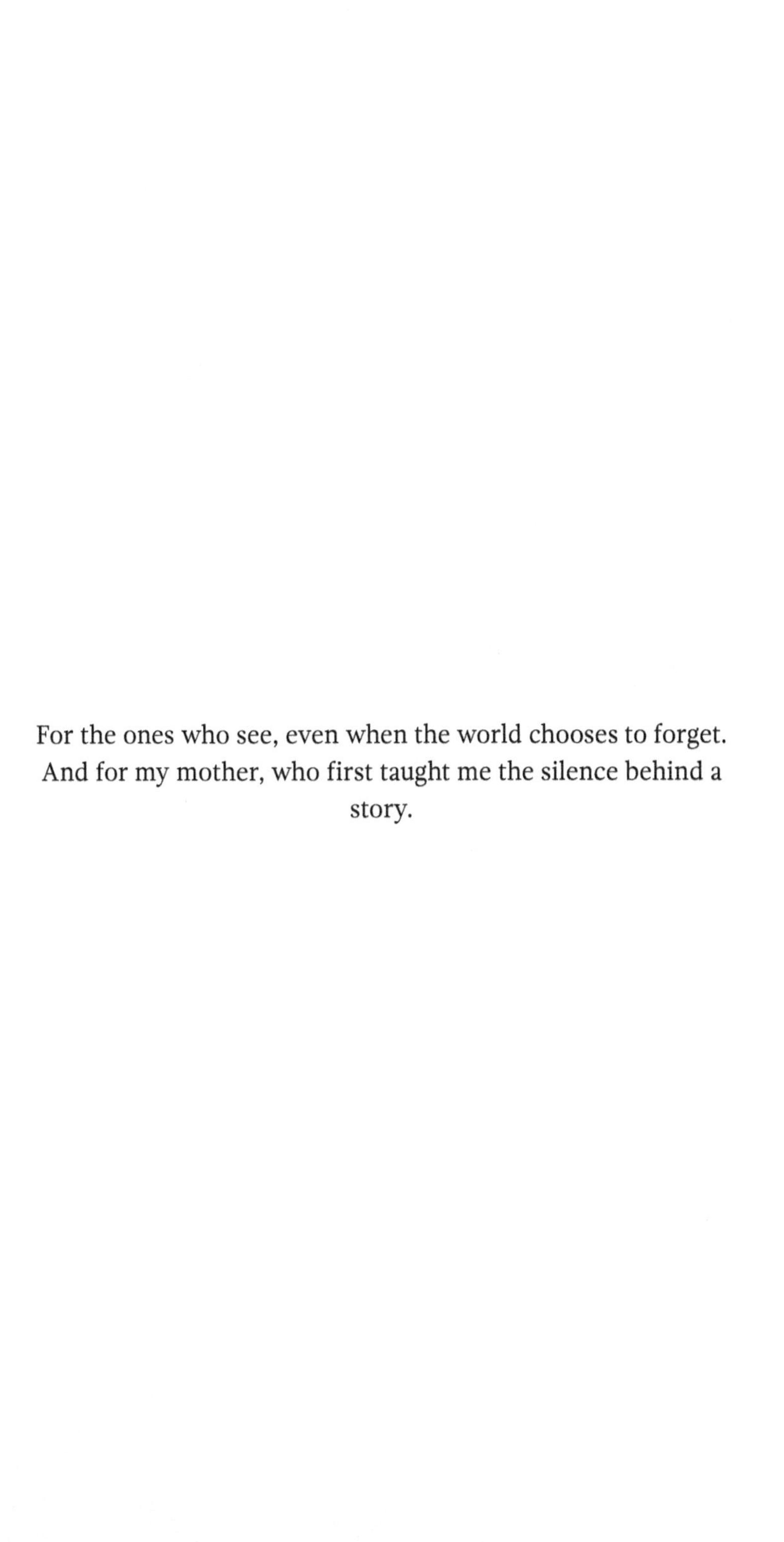

For the ones who see, even when the world chooses to forget.
And for my mother, who first taught me the silence behind a
story.

Contents

Foreword — vii

Preface — ix

Acknowledgements — xi

Prologue — xiii

1. Under The Banyan Sky — 1

2. Rakshasa's Blood — 5

3. The Whispering Teacher — 9

4. Neelashalya's Origin — 13

5. The Cave Of Coiled Memory — 16

6. The Arrow That Waits — 20

7. The Oath Of The Trishula — 23

8. Crossing The Red River — 26

9. The City Of Masks — 29

10. The Forest Of Five Fires — 32

11. The Hermit And The King — 36

12. The Arrow Of The Future — 39

13. The Wind Before The Storm — 42

14. The Council Of Shadows — 45

15. When The Father Returns — 49

16. Threads Of Dharma — 53

17. The War Begins — 57

18. The Head That Watches — 62

19. The Cost Of Silence — 65

20. The Weight Of A Thousand Silent Witnesses — 69

21. The Echoes Of A Kingless Throne — 72

22. The Eternal Witness — 75

Foreword

There are epics we know by heart, of kings and warriors, of battles etched in heaven's memory. But in the vast tapestry of dharma and destiny, there are stories that remain unheard. This is one such story, not of the one who fought, but of the one who could have ended it all, and chose instead to surrender.

Barbarik, the grandson of Bhima, son of Ghatotkacha, is a name that lingers quietly at the edge of the Mahabharata; present, yet hidden. Possessor of the Three Arrows that could pierce through time itself, he stood at the threshold of Kurukshetra not as a warrior, but as a paradox. In his strength lay destruction; in his choice, an eternal question.

Who decides the course of dharma? Is power fulfilled in action, or restraint? And what does it mean to bear witness to a war you were born to stop?

This book is not just a retelling; it is an imagining. A journey into the silences between the verses, into the mind and heart of the boy who became Khatu Shyam. It is rooted in reverence but shaped by reflection, poetic in voice, philosophical in its core.

Barbarik's head may have watched the war. But this tale invites you to see through his eyes, not to judge the victors and the fallen, but to understand the sacred burden of knowing, and the quiet power of sacrifice.

May you read not just with your eyes, but with the stillness of your own inner witness.

Preface

In the vast constellation of the Mahabharata, some stars blaze with renown, Arjuna the peerless archer, Karna the fallen sun, Bhishma the immovable. And yet, there are others who shimmer quietly, their brilliance hidden in silence. Barbarik is one such star.

For generations, his tale has lingered on the fringes of scripture and song, spoken in temples, remembered in ballads, but rarely given the space it deserves in the written word. To many, he is Khatu Shyam, the divine form worshipped across India with unwavering devotion. But before he was a god, he was a boy: a prince of fierce promise, bound by a vow, and faced with a choice no warrior should ever have to make.

This book is my attempt to walk that path with him.

It is not a literal retelling of the Mahabharata, nor a historical chronicle. It is, instead, a literary reimagining, rooted in tradition but shaped by imagination. Through Barbarik's eyes, we witness not just the war of Kurukshetra, but the deeper war within: between justice and attachment, between action and renunciation, between the burden of power and the grace of surrender.

In crafting this narrative, I have sought to retain the tone of an epic, lyrical, immersive, and quietly philosophical. Where scripture is concise, I have ventured into detail; where history is silent, I have listened for echoes. Every liberty taken has been in service of essence, never ego.

To those who know Barbarik as a deity, may this bring you closer to the human heart behind the divine face. And to those meeting him for the first time, may his journey awaken your own reflections on dharma, choice, and what it truly means to bear witness.

With reverence and imagination,

Acknowledgements

To the epics that shaped my imagination; Mahabharata, Ramayana, and countless folk retellings whispered by generations.

To the forests of memory and the winds of language that carried this tale to me.

To those who encouraged the telling of a story both ancient and ever-new.

To all who have stood, like Barbarik, between silence and sacrifice, this is for you.

Prologue

The Hill of Eyes

They placed his head on a mound of red earth, just before the sky cracked open.

A lonely hill, north of Kurukshetra, where no banners flew and no blood was spilled. The wind here did not carry the screams of warriors. It carried silence. Deep, echoing, sacred silence.

And upon that hill sat a single stone pedestal, carved hastily, perhaps in guilt. Upon it, Barbarik's severed head rested with eyes open, unblinking, watching.

The war had begun. But he had already died.

No thunder marked his fall. No *shankha* blew. His bow, Neelashalya, lay coiled in cloth beside the hill, untouched. The quiver that had once held three arrows was empty now, its power returned to the Source.

Barbarik's eyes, though separated from breath, were wide and alive. They glowed faintly, reflecting not the world before him, but something behind it. He saw the battlefields as though through the skin of time. He saw men charging with rage painted on their faces. He saw kings throwing dice inside their hearts. He saw gods seated invisibly in the dust, waiting for choices.

He saw everything.

And yet, there was no hate in his gaze. No judgment. Only a stillness so deep it could swallow the screams of a thousand chariots.

Birds circled above him but did not cry. The sky turned the colour of copper. Clouds gathered like old sages, waiting for a lesson.

And as the first cries of war reached the hill, the head of Barbarik whispered. Not through lips, but through wind, memory, and stone.

"I was not meant to fight.
I was meant to watch.

To remember.
To carry the war after the war was over."
     Thus began the tale of the boy with three arrows.
     The prince of balance.
The warrior of silence.
The eye that saw too much.
     And now, at last, the earth would hear his story.

CHAPTER I

Under the Banyan Sky

Before he was the watcher of the great war, before his name was whispered by winds and remembered in songs, he was a boy who listened to the trees.

The forest of Aranyaka lay beyond the edge of maps, where caravan trails dissolved into deer paths, and the air bore the scent of crushed neem and deep water. At the heart of this forest stood a great banyan tree, vast and ancient, its roots draping the earth like the arms of forgotten sages. Birds nested in its shadows. Spirits, it was said, lingered in its breath.

There, perched upon a smooth branch where the sunlight scattered like gold dust, sat a boy.

His skin held the dusk, neither fair nor dark, but something in between, like the moment just before nightfall. His hair was thick and wild, braided in places by leaves. He sat cross-legged, hands resting on his knees, eyes closed. Not in sleep, but in listening. Not to sound, but to silence.

His name was Barbarik. He was nine years old.

A squirrel leapt past his foot. A koel called from a distance. The banyan stirred with secrets, and the boy seemed to hear every word of it.

"Barbarik" came a sharp voice from below, half-worried, half-stern.

He opened his eyes, a faint smile breaking across his lips.

Down on the forest floor stood a tall woman, her sari wrapped tightly around her legs for easier movement, her dark hair tied with a strip of vine. Her arms were strong, her eyes stronger.

Morvi.

His mother.

Not queen, though she had once been called so. Not Rakshasi, though her bloodline was from that clan of warriors who ran with wolves and vanished into mist. Here, she was simply mother.

"You've been gone since sunrise," she said, tilting her head. "Again."

"The tree was telling me a story" Barbarik replied, swinging down from the branch with the ease of a monkey.

She raised an eyebrow. "Did it also tell you that breakfast has turned to ash and the goat has chewed through the rice basket?"

He grinned. "Then the goat is wiser than we think."

Morvi smirked in spite of herself. "Come."

They walked together through the underbrush, weaving between sal trees and curling roots. The hut they returned to was simple - wood, mud, and leaf-thatch - yet something about it felt sacred. It stood by a small stream and faced east, as Morvi insisted every home must. Nearby sat Chitti, the one-horned goat, chewing with divine indifference.

Inside the hut, a clay stove hissed. Above it hung a painted scroll, faded but beautiful, depicting a blue-skinned man with a mace, riding a cloud.

Barbarik paused before it, as he often did.

"Is that Grandfather Bhima?" he asked, half-whispering.

Morvi looked at the painting for a moment. "Yes. As I saw him once, in the rain, before your father marched into battle."

Barbarik nodded slowly.

He had never met Bhima.

He had never met his father, Ghatotkacha, either.

But he had heard stories. So many stories.

Of Ghatotkacha, the mountain-shadow with wings of thunder, who was said to command the very storm clouds, whose roars turned fleeing armies into legends, and whose presence on the battlefield would surely be felt like thunder given form.

Of Bhima, the mighty Pandava, who crushed elephants with his bare hands and dined with demons without flinching.

And of Hidimbi, his grandmother, who left her people to walk beside love.

"But they were all warriors," Barbarik said suddenly, looking up. "And I?"

Morvi turned to him, kneeling to his height. "You are more than a warrior," she said. "You are what comes after one."

His eyes searched hers. "What does that mean?"

"It means strength is your gift," she said, placing a hand on his chest, "but compassion is your duty. You carry both human and Rakshasa blood - but you are bound by something deeper than lineage."

"What?"

She smiled. "Balance."

Just then, a crow cried thrice in the distance.

Morvi stiffened slightly. "That's near the stone ridge," she said. "Wait here."

But Barbarik had already picked up the bow he had carved from the fallen limb of a neem tree, notched with a single reed arrow.

"I'll come," he said simply.

Morvi studied him. Then nodded.

They walked together through the thinning trees, toward the stone ridge that marked the edge of their forest domain. As they crested the hill, they saw them.

Three travellers' dust-covered, armed with sickles and torches. Hunting something.

Morvi's eyes narrowed. "Poachers."

Barbarik stepped forward.

But she held him back. "Not yet."

Then, without warning, a cry rang out; a shrill, panicked bleat.

Chitti!

They had found her.

Morvi tensed. But Barbarik had already moved.

He ran like wind over stone. His feet barely touched the earth. The poachers turned just as he appeared, small, barefoot, unarmed but for a curved stick.

They laughed.

And then, the wind shifted.

The boy's eyes turned darker. Not cruel, but old.

He moved. Fast. Too fast.

The reed arrow struck the leader's torch from his hand. The second poacher dropped his sickle, clutching his wrist as if struck by thunder. The third turned to run, and fell, tripped by a root that hadn't been there a moment before.

When Morvi arrived, breathless, all three were on the ground gasping, unhurt but shaken, as if the forest itself had turned against them.

Barbarik stood beside Chitti, gently stroking her flank.

The poachers fled without a word.

Morvi looked at her son, not afraid, but quiet.

"You didn't touch them."

"No," he said.

"You could have."

"I could have."

"Then why didn't you?"

Barbarik's answer came soft and sure:

"Because I saw their fear before they showed their cruelty. And because I knew they would leave."

She watched him, then really watched him.

And in that moment, she knew:

The forest had done its part. It had shaped the boy.

But the time was near.

He would need a teacher now.

And the world was waiting.

CHAPTER II

Rakshasa's Blood

The moon rose silver over Aranyaka, veiled in clouds that drifted like forgotten thoughts. Insects chirred in the underbrush, and the night pulsed with its own quiet rhythm. Somewhere in the dark, an owl called twice.

Barbarik sat outside the hut, legs folded beneath him, his fingers tracing symbols into the dust, curves and dots that only he seemed to understand. His eyes were distant. Not in sleep. In thought.

He had not spoken much since the incident with the poachers.

Morvi watched him from the doorway. The fire behind her cast soft shadows against the clay walls. In one hand, she held a bowl of warm milk spiced with ginger and honey. In the other, a woven cloth.

"You're still awake," she said gently, stepping outside.

"The banyan won't sleep tonight," Barbarik murmured.

Morvi followed his gaze. The great tree stood in the distance, lit only by moonlight, its leaves rustling like the whispers of old ghosts.

She sat beside him and offered the bowl. He took it silently, sipped once, then held it between his palms.

"I frightened them," he said at last.

"Yes," Morvi replied. "You did."

"I didn't mean to."

"I know."

There was a pause.

"Am I like them?" he asked. "The rakshasas?"

Morvi exhaled. The question had arrived sooner than she had hoped.

"You are of them," she said carefully. "But you are not them."

Barbarik looked up. "Then what am I?"

She didn't answer immediately. Instead, she unfolded the cloth she had brought and laid it across his lap.

It was old. Faded. But still beautiful.

An embroidered banner, the threads stitched with the patience of long nights. Upon it, the crest of a forgotten clan: a winged boar, leaping through flames.

"Your father wore this," she said. "When he left for the war."

Barbarik touched the fabric as if it might vanish.

"Did he ever return?" he asked.

Morvi's gaze drifted to the treetops, where the wind carried nothing but silence.

"No," she said gently. "Not yet."

He turned to her. "Was he a monster too?"

Morvi's eyes flashed, not with anger, but with something deeper.

"Do not let the world name what it does not understand. Your father was a warrior. A protector. A son of the forest and the storm. He was born of Rakshasa blood, yes, but he walked in dharma."

"And his mother?" Barbarik asked. "The one who left her clan?"

"Hidimbi," she said, nodding. "Your grandmother."

She let the word linger in the night.

"She was fierce," Morvi continued. "Wise, too. She challenged Bhima in combat, and chose him in love. She led her people with grace. After Bhima left, she raised Ghatotkacha alone. As I have raised you."

Barbarik was quiet.

The forest rustled around them.

And then, as if something inside him cracked open:

"Sometimes, when I am angry, I feel it rise."

Morvi didn't speak.

"It coils in my belly," he went on. "Like smoke. It wants to break things. Hurt things."

Her hand found his shoulder.

"That is the Rakshasa," she said. "The fire we carry in our blood."

"I try to push it down."

"No," she said firmly. "Do not push it down. Learn its name. Know its face. Make it kneel to you."

He looked at her, eyes wide. "Can it be done?"

"Yes," she said. "But not here. Not by me."

He blinked. "Then who?"

A shadow passed over the moon. The wind shifted.

"There is someone," she said. "A seer. A warrior. Neither man nor beast. They live beyond the seven hills. They once taught your father, before the war came. If they still live."

Barbarik's heart stirred. "Can I go?"

"Not yet," she said. "First, you must be tested."

"By whom?"

She smiled faintly. "By the forest."

At that, the air grew suddenly heavy, like the moments before a storm.

"Come," she said, rising. "It is time."

They walked into the woods, deeper than he had ever gone, past trees that no longer bore names, past stones covered in moss shaped like old runes.

Finally, they came to a clearing.

In the centre stood a stone pillar, cracked with age, wrapped in vines. Upon it sat three objects: a bowl of ash, a copper mirror, and a carved mask of a Rakshasa, its eyes wide, its fangs bared, its mouth locked in a scream.

Morvi pointed.

"You will face the mask," she said. "But you will not fight it. You will enter it."

Barbarik hesitated. "What do you mean?"

"Close your eyes. Breathe. Sit before it. And listen."

He obeyed.

The night deepened.

And as he breathed, the world tilted.

He felt himself falling, not down, but inward. Into the silence behind thought. Into a place where trees had no leaves and his skin was not his own.

He stood in a great hall of mirrors.

But none showed his face.

In one, he saw a beast of tusks and flame. In another, a boy holding a bloodied sword. In the third, nothing at all.

The mirrors began to tremble.

Then speak.

One voice.

Many mouths.

"Who are you?"

He opened his mouth to answer

And woke.

Gasping.

Covered in sweat.

The clearing was still. The mask sat silent. But the bowl of ash was now smoking.

Morvi stood nearby, unreadable.

Barbarik rose.

"What did you see?" she asked.

"Myself," he said.

"Which one?"

He met her gaze.

"All of them."

And for the first time, Morvi smiled.

"You are ready."

CHAPTER III

The Whispering Teacher

The morning mist curled low over the earth like the breath of slumbering spirits. Dew clung to every leaf, every web, every blade of grass with a tenderness that seemed reluctant to let go. And yet, go it must.

Barbarik stood at the edge of the forest clearing where Morvi had tested him. In his satchel were dried berries, smoked root, a small vial of rainwater, and the piece of embroidered cloth with the winged boar, his father's crest. Morvi had packed them silently at dawn, her fingers moving with care, her eyes unreadable.

"You are not going to find answers," she had told him as they embraced. "You are going to lose the questions."

Now, alone, he stepped beyond the trees he had always known. Every footfall was a farewell. The soil here had a different scent, older, deeper, almost sweet. The light filtered through unfamiliar branches. Somewhere above, an unseen bird called in a language he didn't yet understand.

He followed no path.

There were none.

Morvi had told him, "You will not find the Guru. If the time is right, the Guru will find you."

So he walked.

For two days and three nights he wandered, sleeping beneath the stars, listening to the hush of unseen beasts and the sighing of old trees. On the fourth morning, as he chewed a bitter berry and watched a family of deer vanish into the fog, he heard it.

A whisper.

Faint. Drawn-out. Not in words. In presence.

Like a thought spoken by the forest itself.

It came again.

Not through his ears. Through his bones.

"Turn left."

He did.

And suddenly, the trees were different.

Thinner. Taller. Silver-barked and bare, rising like spears into the sky. The air grew cool. Hushed. The very ground seemed to soften beneath his feet.

There was a clearing ahead.

At its centre sat a figure on a great stone.

Not man.

Not beast.

Something in between.

The creature's skin was the grey of smoke. Its hair fell in coils like vines. A single eye gleamed from the centre of its forehead. Its body was garlanded in feathers, bones, and bells. It looked at Barbarik as if it had known him before birth.

"You took long enough," the creature said.

Its voice was neither male nor female. It carried the clarity of a flute and the weight of thunder.

Barbarik swallowed. "Are you the Guru?"

"I am one," the creature said, "who remembers what others have forgotten. Names. Songs. The shape of rage before it becomes war."

Barbarik bowed low. "I seek to learn."

"No," the Guru said. "You seek to master."

Barbarik looked up. "Is that wrong?"

"It is unnecessary," the Guru replied. "The tiger does not master its claws. It remembers it has them."

Barbarik hesitated. "Then, will you teach me?"

"I will test you."

The air trembled.

Without moving, the Guru raised one finger.

From the trees, a shadow leapt.

Barbarik barely had time to breathe.

A beast landed before him, hulking, black-furred, four arms, eyes like molten gold. Its mouth opened in a howl that shook the leaves. It charged.

He dodged left, rolled, grabbed a fallen branch, and struck its knee. It buckled, roared, and swiped. He ducked. The wind of the blow stung his face.

"Do not run," the Guru's voice came. "Do not fight."

Barbarik blinked. The branch in his hand burned.

"Then what?"

The beast lunged again.

He closed his eyes.

And remembered.

The mask in the clearing.

The mirrors.

The beast of tusks and flame.

He opened his arms.

The monster collided into him, and passed through.

Like mist.

Barbarik stumbled but did not fall.

He turned.

The beast was gone.

Only silence.

And the Guru's voice.

"Very good."

Barbarik looked up. "What was that?"

"Your fear," the Guru said. "Wrapped in teeth."

They stepped down from the stone, towering now, close enough that Barbarik could smell the herbs braided into its hair.

"You will stay here," the Guru said. "Until the roots of your rage grow flowers."

Barbarik nodded.

The Guru reached into a pouch and pulled out a bow.

It was not made of wood.

It shimmered like deep river water. Carved from a single horn of some ancient creature. Its string was braided lightning. Its name was carved in old script across the limb: Neelashalya, the Blue Thorn.

Barbarik reached for it.

The Guru pulled it away.
"Not yet," they said. "You must earn it."
"How?"
The Guru smiled, a slow, wide smile with too many teeth.
"You will know."
And thus began the long learning.

CHAPTER IV

Neelashalya's Origin

The days in the Guru's grove passed without numbers. Time stretched like tree bark, layered, slow, fragrant with meaning. The silver forest stood timeless around them, ageless and unbound. Barbarik woke with the sun, slept when the moon whispered lullabies through the canopy, and trained in between 'flesh, thought, and spirit' until he no longer knew where one ended and the other began.

He was not taught in words alone.

The Guru would sit, still as a stone, and expect him to listen to the wind. To drink silence like broth. To move like breath through flame. When Barbarik questioned, he was met with riddles. When he obeyed, the forest seemed to nod.

One evening, after a long and silent trance beneath the roots of a singing fig tree, the Guru brought out the bow again.

Neelashalya.

It gleamed in the moonlight, a soft, deep azure that was not of any earthly hue. It seemed liquid at first glance, solid only when you looked away. The string whispered. Not in sound, but in emotion. Anticipation. Hunger. Memory.

Barbarik's fingers reached toward it instinctively.

The Guru pulled it back once more. "Do you know what you are reaching for?"

"I know it is mine," he said.

"Not yet," the Guru replied. "First, know what it is."

And they began to tell the tale.

"In the first age," the Guru said, voice slow as dusk, "before men built kingdoms and gods took sides, there lived a beast whose blood sang louder than war drums. A horned serpent it was, half creature, half curse. Its breath scorched valleys. Its cry caused rivers to forget their direction. The rishis called it Shalya - as in thorn - because it pierced dharma wherever it crawled."

"None could kill it. No army could cage it. It was not evil, nor good, it simply was. Hunger made flesh."

"One day, a woman came."

"Who?" Barbarik asked.

"No one remembers," the Guru replied. "Some say she was a warrior. Others, a forest witch. Some call her the Mother of Moonlight. She was nameless. She was alone."

"She did not fight the beast."

"She sang to it."

Barbarik blinked. "Sang?"

The Guru nodded. "For seven nights. No weapon drawn. No trap set. Only voice and truth. She told the serpent stories, of pain, of patience, of stars forgotten. On the eighth dawn, the creature bowed its head and laid down its horn."

The Guru gently placed the bow in Barbarik's hands.

"This is that horn."

Barbarik stared, reverently.

"But, how does it still live?" he whispered.

"It does not live. It remembers. The spirit of the serpent, the hunger, was not destroyed. It was bound."

"To the bow?"

"To the wielder."

Barbarik looked up sharply.

"You mean?"

"Yes," the Guru said. "To wield Neelashalya is to be chosen by the beast's memory. It listens. It learns your rage. It shapes it. If you are unworthy, it turns on you."

Barbarik swallowed.

"It will not obey your strength," the Guru continued. "Only your silence. Your clarity. The serpent bowed only to song."

"And the arrows?"

"They are not mere weapons. They are truths."

The Guru brought forth a small box, old as soil.

Inside lay three arrows - each of a different hue.

The first gleamed silver-blue, cool and clean like mountain spring. "This one marks the deserving."

The second pulsed crimson, like still blood. "This one destroys the marked."

The third was jet black, so dark it seemed to drink the light around it. "And this one sees all that stands between the two."

Barbarik's hands trembled as he touched them.

"But they are bound," the Guru said. "To Neelashalya. And Neelashalya is not yet yours."

Barbarik looked up. "Then what must I do?"

The Guru smiled, deep and unreadable.

"Offer your hunger. In the cave beyond the black banyan. There, the serpent waits, not in body, but in memory. If you return with silence, the bow will accept you."

Barbarik nodded.

And that night, he walked alone, bearing no weapon, only the tale in his heart.

He stepped into the mouth of the cave.

It breathed him in.

CHAPTER V

The Cave of Coiled Memory

The cave yawned wide like the mouth of an ancient god, dark, indifferent, full of breathless depth. As Barbarik stepped past the moss-covered maw, the forest behind him seemed to fall away. No birds called. No breeze stirred. Even his heartbeat seemed to hush in deference to the place.

He carried no torch.

The darkness was total, yet not blinding. It pulsed faintly, as if lit from within by old memory. As he moved forward, the very rock underfoot felt warm, not from fire, but from recollection, like stone that remembered sunlight long gone.

He did not know how long he walked.

Time, in that place, had no bones.

Then, as if summoned by his stillness, the voice came.

Not loud.

Not even spoken.

Just known.

"Why do you seek the thorn?"

Barbarik did not speak aloud. He did not know how. His thoughts unfurled like cloth, offered willingly.

"To protect those who cannot protect themselves."

"Lies!"

He flinched.

"You seek power."

He bowed his head. "I do."

You seek vengeance.

"I do not deny it."

"You seek to make war fair."

He hesitated. "Yes."

The silence that followed was not approval. It was amusement.

"There is no fairness in war, child of Bhima. There is only weight. And price. And the grief of the living."

Barbarik breathed deeply. "Then I will bear the weight."

A sound like rustling scales filled the air.

And suddenly, the darkness moved.

It was not shadow.

It was the serpent.

Coiled around the cavern walls, loop upon loop, impossibly vast, its eyes were two molten rings of starlight. Its mouth was closed, but its presence spoke.

"Do you remember me?"

Barbarik blinked. "I, no."

"Your blood does."

And as the serpent's gaze pierced him, Barbarik fell, not bodily, but inward, through a flood of vision.

He was a soldier in a war long forgotten, bearing a broken banner, his eyes bloodshot, his hands slick with guilt.

He was a beast, cornered and wounded, watching a village burn as his kin were slain.

He was a child, clutching his mother's body as marauders laughed.

And in each vision, rage bloomed.

Not his own.

But old.

Ancient.

Shared.

He gasped, returning to himself, drenched in cold sweat. The serpent had not moved.

"I am not your enemy," the voice said. "I am your echo."

"What must I do?" Barbarik whispered.

"Show me your silence."

Barbarik closed his eyes.

He inhaled once. Deep.

And let go.

Of pain.

Of names.

Of desire to prove, to punish, to be seen.

He became breath.

Still.

A single, steady pulse in the heart of the world.

The silence was vast.

The serpent uncoiled, slowly, reverently.

Its form shimmered, then faded, becoming light, becoming dust, becoming breath again.

And from that light, something emerged.

The bow.

Neelashalya.

Floating before him, as if cradled in moonlight.

He reached out.

Touched it.

It did not burn.

It hummed.

And from above, a single droplet of silver fell and landed on his brow.

A mark not of war, but of readiness.

When Barbarik stepped out of the cave, the forest was waiting.

The Guru sat beneath the black banyan.

They smiled.

"You did not slay the beast," they said.

"No," Barbarik replied. "I listened."

"Then Neelashalya is yours."

The bow rested on his back, silent and watchful.

"And the arrows?"

"When the time comes," the Guru said, "they will find their path."

And with that, the training began anew, not of the body, but of burden. How to see with clarity. How to choose the marked. How to let go, even when power surged.

For Barbarik was no longer a boy with strength.

He was now a wielder of memory.

And memory had teeth.

CHAPTER VI

The Arrow That Waits

It was the black arrow that troubled Barbarik the most.

The silver one gleamed like justice unflinching, clear. The crimson one pulsed with finality an end that could not be undone. But the third... the third arrow neither shimmered nor called. It simply watched.

And waited.

The Guru placed it before him one quiet dusk, on a slab of redwood beside the lotus pond. Neelashalya rested beside it, coiled in its own silence.

"The arrow of knowledge," the Guru said. "The one that sees."

Barbarik bowed his head. "What does it seek?"

"Everything," the Guru replied. "Doubt. Deceit. Intention. Truth buried beneath skin and gesture. Before the other two fly, this one must know."

Barbarik frowned. "But I already know who the unjust are. I can see it in their eyes."

The Guru turned, slow and measured. "Then you are not ready to use this."

They walked to the grove's edge, where a young deer lay caught in a thorn trap a cruel device left by poachers from the far valley. Barbarik bent swiftly, untying the snare with ease, comforting the trembling fawn. His fingers moved with purpose. Mercy, even.

The Guru watched.

Then asked, "Would you slay the one who laid the trap?"

Barbarik rose. "Yes. Without hesitation."

"And if the man had done so to feed his starving child?"

He paused.

"If he had been cast out by kings, with no land to till, no voice to speak with?"

Barbarik's jaw tightened. "He still harmed the innocent."

"And yet," said the Guru, "you would condemn him before knowing why he became what he is?"

Barbarik looked down.

The black arrow still lay there, untouched.

"It does not kill," the Guru said. "It waits. It learns. It humbles."

Barbarik whispered, "Then how do I wield it?"

"You do not," the Guru said. "It chooses when it must be released."

That night, Barbarik dreamt of a village burning.

Not in conquest but in confusion. Friend turned on friend. Brother on brother. All claimed righteousness. All pointed at each other with trembling hands.

In the centre of it all stood Barbarik, Neelashalya drawn, arrows glowing at his back.

He lifted the silver arrow.

They cried for justice.

He nocked the crimson one.

They screamed of vengeance.

And then he reached for the black arrow.

It refused to rise.

He stood frozen, uncertain.

The fire raged.

And when he awoke, his palms were wet with sweat.

The following day, the Guru gave him no weapons. Only a question.

"There are two kings," they said. "Each claims the other wronged him. Each offers gold and song for your loyalty. Both plead for help."

Barbarik narrowed his eyes. "Who is right?"

"That," said the Guru, "is what you must find. And you must do so without sword, arrow, or threat. You have three days."

And so Barbarik walked.

He watched one king feed orphans by day and plan conquest by night.

He watched the other pray at dawn and tax the poor by dusk.

He listened to weavers, warriors, widows.

He watched children chase one another in the shadow of bitter palaces.

When he returned, he sat quietly.

The Guru did not ask.

Barbarik spoke.

"I could not choose."

"Why?"

"Because neither was just. And neither was a villain. Only… broken."

The Guru smiled faintly.

"Then you begin to understand."

Barbarik looked toward the place where the black arrow was kept.

It glowed faintly, for the first time.

In the weeks that followed, he trained not with blade or bow but with questions. He learned to read not just faces, but silences. He spoke less. Heard more.

The black arrow remained with him.

Not in hand.

In thought.

It did not seek to strike.

It sought to witness.

Thus Barbarik's training neared completion not in skill, which he already possessed, but in judgment, which he was learning to bear.

One arrow to reveal the deserving.

One to strike with finality.

And one to teach him that sometimes, the greatest act of power

Was to wait.

CHAPTER VII

The Oath of the Trishula

The winds of Vaishantagiri were not like those of the forest. They did not whisper. They did not hum. They howled clear, high, and full of silence so vast that even a god might hesitate to speak.

Barbarik stood at the edge of the sky.

Behind him, the path wound up through bamboo thickets, neem groves, and narrow cliffs. Before him, three stone steps rose from the mountaintop to a circular dais carved with old glyphs too ancient for even the Guru to name. At the dais "™s center stood the Trishula: a great three-pronged spear of blackened bronze, its shaft etched with flame and river, its tips kissed by lightning.

It had no guards.

It needed none.

The Trishula belonged not to any warrior but to Dharma itself.

And on that cold, breathless summit, Barbarik was to take the oath.

The Guru stood beside him, their robes billowing like smoke in the wind. They carried no staff. No scroll.

Only a single bell of copper, slung by cord from one wrist.

"You may still turn back," they said, voice low but firm.

Barbarik shook his head.

"Then go," said the Guru, and stepped away.

Alone, Barbarik ascended the three steps. Each one felt like a century.

The air shimmered.

Not with heat.

With memory.

At the first step, he saw a battlefield not future, not past, but eternal. Spears driven into ash. Shields broken. Voices crying for names long forgotten.

From the dust rose a question: "Will you choose knowledge before judgment?"

Barbarik placed his foot forward.

Yes.

The image vanished.

At the second step, he saw a woman shielding a child from a sword. The sword trembled. The wielder wept. And still the blow had to fall.

From the blood came a whisper: Will you bear the weight of those you cannot save?

He inhaled.

Yes.

The wind screamed once and died.

At the third step, nothing rose.

Only stillness.

And then a voice not from the air, not from the earth, but from within:

Will you die before you are known?

He closed his eyes.

And said:

Yes.

The dais responded.

The wind circled inward, like a tide reversing.

The Trishula glowed not with light, but with presence.

A circle of flame etched itself beneath Barbarik's feet silent fire, cool to the touch.

From the sky fell three petals: one gold, one blue, one crimson.

They landed on his palms, and turned to ash.

The Guru rang the copper bell once.

Its echo did not end.

It simply became part of the air.

"You have taken the oath," they said, stepping forward. "From this day, you are no longer only son, or student. You are Vratadhari oath-bound. You must now walk alone."

Barbarik bowed.

"But I am not alone," he said.

Neelashalya pulsed at his back.

The three arrows shimmered in their quivers.

And the wind, for just a moment, turned gentle.

That night, at the edge of the fire, the Guru spoke for the last time.

"When you reach the field of war, you will see not enemies and allies but threads. Some bound in truth. Some in ambition. Some knotted in suffering so tight they do not know how to unbind."

Barbarik nodded.

"And what shall I do?"

The Guru smiled.

"Be the hand that does not tremble. But more than that be the heart that does not close."

And with that, they faded into the trees, the copper bell silent.

Barbarik stood alone.

But he was ready.

CHAPTER VIII

Crossing the Red River

The mountains ended not with a drop, but with a sigh.

Barbarik stood at the crest of the final ridge, where pine gave way to scrub, and wild orchids surrendered to thorn bush. Below him sprawled the great plain of Kuru dusty, golden, and restless. Villages dotted the landscape like anklet bells on the feet of a dancer forever in motion.

And cutting through it all like a scar of rust was the Red River Raktavahini, as the old bards had called it. The blood-carrier. In its waters, kings had drowned. On its banks, treaties had died. And somewhere beyond that river, the drums of war were beginning to speak.

Barbarik's shadow stretched long behind him, crowned with the shape of his bow, Neelashalya.

He did not turn back.

The descent was slow.

He passed shepherds with sorrow in their eyes, temples with doors shut tight, and fig trees festooned with torn flags each a prayer, each unanswered.

In one village, a mother sprinkled turmeric at his feet, mistaking him for a god. He knelt and returned the gesture, saying nothing.

In another, children ran from him not in fear, but awe. "Is he a Yaksha? " one whispered. "A Kshatriya with demon eyes? " another asked. Their elders pulled them away, murmuring about omens and stars falling from the east.

He did not stop them. He had seen this before. The forest taught him: the world loves the idea of power, until it walks among them.

By the fifth night, he reached the river.

The Raktavahini.

It flowed sluggish and wide, like molten iron beneath a twilight sky. Reeds stood tall like sentinels. Egrets circled, solemn and still.

No bridge spanned its width. Only an old stone boat waited half-submerged, moss-ridden, tied to a post carved with names worn smooth by time.

He stepped in.

The boat did not creak.

The waters lapped once, and began to carry him.

Halfway across, the sky split open.

Not with rain but fire.

A trail of smoke raced across the heavens a comet, burning red, trailing sparks like tongues of a forgotten curse. It arced from east to west, vanishing behind the hills.

Barbarik's eyes narrowed.

And then came the sound.

Not thunder.

Not wind.

But the clash of steel.

Faint, distant, real.

He had heard no armies. No conch shells. No banners flapping in the air. And yet the war had already begun beyond sight, but not beyond consequence.

The boat nudged the far bank.

He stepped onto dry land.

And the ground felt different.

Not hostile.

But waiting.

That night, he found an abandoned shrine to Vayu, the Wind-Lord his great-grandfather. The shrine had no roof. Its idol had crumbled into a heap of cracked stone and vine. But a single diya still flickered within, sheltered by a rusted bowl.

He knelt.

Not to pray.

To remember.

He remembered stories of Bhima the giant who had broken elephants with his arms. Of his own father, Ghatotkacha, whose feet never touched the earth in battle. Of his grandmother, Hidimba, and her eyes like moonlight in a cave.

And then he remembered his vow.

"To fight on the side of the just. To take no more than three arrows. To end the war with only three strikes, should I choose."

He had taken the vow in silence.

But tonight, he spoke it aloud.

And the flame in the diya did not flicker.

In the forest behind the shrine, someone watched.

A man in grey robes, hair coiled like a serpent on his head. A scroll of birchbark in one hand. A dagger in the other.

He turned to the shadows and whispered, "He has crossed."

Another voice, dry as old leather, answered, "Then the sons of Kuru will soon know fear."

"Which one shall he serve?" the man asked.

There was no reply.

Only the rustle of a hundred wings taking flight.

Barbarik, unaware, slept with Neelashalya by his side, the three arrows laid before him like stars fallen from their constellations.

The war had not yet begun.

But the world had already changed.

CHAPTER IX

The City of Masks

Dawn rose not with light but with noise.

The city of Avighna stirred like a serpent shedding sleep. Markets unfurled. Horns blared. Brass bells clanged from temples while conches boomed from towers. In every alleyway, smoke curled upward incense from shrines, steam from kitchens, dust from carts. It was a city alive and hungry, its appetite fed by the rumour of war.

Barbarik entered through the eastern gate, a tall arc of black basalt engraved with the seven seals of ancient kings. Nobody stopped him. Nobody dared. In a place where merchants disguised themselves as mendicants, and spies as poets, a tall youth cloaked in mountain wool, a sapphire bow slung across his back, and eyes that shimmered with storm was just another story waiting to be bartered.

He walked without fear. But not without notice.

In Avighna, every corner had ears.

And they had already heard of him.

A boy approached first a beggar with no shoes and one cloudy eye. He circled Barbarik thrice, muttering.

"You come from the hills. From the path of oaths. That bow, what is it called?"

"Neelashalya," said Barbarik.

The boy grinned, showing a missing tooth. "The blue thorn. Sharp. But not cruel. Like moonlight hiding a blade."

He darted off before Barbarik could speak again.

From a rooftop above, a veiled woman dropped a marigold. It landed at his feet.

He looked up.

She was gone.

By midday, the stories had swelled like a monsoon-fed river.

A lone warrior has come.

He walks with three arrows and a silent vow.

He has no master, no army.

Not yet.

And so, they came.

The first was a merchant of spices so he claimed who offered Barbarik a hundred horses in exchange for one arrow. "A sample," he smiled, "for appraisal, not war."

Barbarik declined.

The second was a Bhargava priest, face smeared in holy ash. "Let your vow be judged by Agni. I will test you in fire." His eyes gleamed too brightly. Barbarik walked past.

The third, cloaked in indigo, spoke plainly. "The sons of Kuru await you. They know of your oath. They fear it. And will strike first, if you do not choose."

Barbarik stopped. "I have not chosen."

"Then choose soon," the man said. "In war, the undecided are the first to fall."

He vanished into the crowd.

Barbarik found shelter in an old potter's shed near the city's edge. The potter, a quiet man with a limp and a flute tucked behind his ear, asked no questions. He pointed to a cot of straw, handed Barbarik a bowl of warm millet, and returned to shaping a lump of red clay into a lamp.

Barbarik ate in silence.

That night, he dreamt.

He stood in a hall of mirrors.

Each one showed a version of himself.

One bathed in blood, a crown of fire upon his brow.

Another walking alone through ash, Neelashalya broken.

A third, kneeling in dust before a woman in white, weeping as the sky rained arrows.

The mirrors cracked. One by one. Until only a single pane remained.

It showed no image. Only darkness.

And from that darkness came a whisper:

"Choose.

Not who you will fight.

But who you will become."

He woke before dawn.

Avighna was still.

Even the crows had gone quiet.

Barbarik stepped into the street.

And saw them.

Two riders, cloaked in grey, waiting beneath a banyan. Their mounts restless. Their eyes unreadable.

"Come," one said. "The southern camp moves at daybreak. Yudhisthira summons you."

"And if I do not come?"

"Then others will."

The riders turned.

Barbarik did not follow.

Not yet.

He turned back to the potter, who now stood at the doorway with folded arms.

"You knew," said Barbarik.

The potter nodded. "Even a broken flute knows music when it hears it."

"What would you do?"

"I would listen," the potter said. "To the sound beneath the silence."

Barbarik stepped away from the city gates.

Beyond them, the plains opened wide. One path to Hastinapura. Another to the Pandava camp. A third, winding and uncertain, leading to the forest of Kurujangala, where ancient rishis still kept watch over truth.

He did not yet choose.

But he walked forward.

And the road, it seemed, chose him.

CHAPTER X

The Forest of Five Fires

The sun was still low when Barbarik entered Kurujangala a place older than cities and kings, where trees grew tall without fear, and winds moved like whispers from another age. This was no ordinary forest. Sages had come here to burn away the remnants of ego. Warriors had come to lose their names.

Barbarik came as neither. Not yet.

He came walking, not riding. His bow, Neelashalya, was slung across his back, its string unstrung in deference to the silence of the trees. His three arrows were wrapped in cloth, bound like a promise he had not yet fully understood. The path he followed was not a path at all only the urging of something deeper than instinct, quieter than thought.

Birdsong faded as he moved deeper. Even beasts that ruled other forests watched him from a distance, neither fearing nor challenging him. The forest knew the scent of his bloodline. It had once known another who bore it.

On the third day, he came upon the first fire. It hovered above a small stone pool, flickering without fuel or smoke, as if it had burned since the world began.

He folded his hands and bowed.

The second flame blazed atop a black rock shaped like a crouching lion. The third danced beneath the roots of an ancient banyan, its light reflecting in a still stream. The fourth curled in a hollow beneath the earth, where no wind reached and no leaf dared fall.

The fifth was nowhere to be seen.

Instead, from behind the banyan's curtain of roots, an old man emerged. His robes were woven from bark and dusk. His beard reached his knees, and his eyes shone like still water at night.

"You've found four," the old man said. "And you've kept silence before them. That is not common."

Barbarik lowered his head, but said nothing.

The old man nodded, pleased. "Very well. The fifth fire will not show itself to those who seek only power. Come."

He turned and walked deeper into the woods. Barbarik followed.

They passed trees that leaned as if listening. Stones along the way bore markings in no known script. The air grew warmer. Not from sunlight, but from something within the forest itself.

They stopped at a clearing where only ash remained. No shrine, no smoke. Just a wide circle of scorched earth, blackened long ago.

"This was where the fifth burned," the sage said. "It appears only when one stands at a turning. When choice weighs heavier than certainty."

Barbarik looked around. "What choice?"

The sage smiled faintly. "The kind you don't yet know you're making."

And then, without any sign or sound, a figure stepped from the shadows of the trees.

He was tall, his skin deep as rainclouds, his chest bare but adorned with a necklace of bones and tiger-teeth. His hair fell in matted locks over his shoulders. His eyes were quiet thunder.

Barbarik's breath caught.

He had never seen his father.

But he had seen paintings images drawn by wandering bards and described by his mother with reverence. The figure before him could only be one.

"Ghatotkacha," the sage said, "Son of Bhima. Warrior of the northern heights."

The figure smiled, but it was not a smile of welcome. It held gravity, the kind borne by those who had seen too many deaths to treat meeting as reunion.

Barbarik stepped forward, uncertain. "You're alive."

Ghatotkacha's voice rumbled low. "Of course I am."

"Then why?" Barbarik swallowed. "Why did you never return?"

"I fought where I was needed. I watched from afar. Your path was not to be guided by my shadow. But today, the forest asked me to step into it for you."

Barbarik looked at the ash-ringed clearing. "Is this some test?"

"No," Ghatotkacha said. "This is a moment. One that will shape you more than any weapon ever will."

He walked closer, and his presence filled the space like approaching rain.

"You wonder whether you carry my blood or my burden. You wonder if you are a monster hiding in flesh, or a warrior hiding from war. I cannot give you the answers. But I can give you the truth."

Barbarik's eyes did not flinch. "Say it."

"We are born of two natures, you and I. The world will fear one and demand the other. But you must hold both, not choose between them. Only then will you understand the meaning of your arrows."

Silence.

Then something stirred in the ash. A tiny ember flickered at the centre of the circle. Another joined it. Then a curl of smoke.

The fifth fire breathed again.

It rose not tall, but steady like a heart remembering its rhythm.

Barbarik turned toward it. Ghatotkacha watched him, arms folded.

"You are ready," the older warrior said. "But not finished."

"Will I see you again?"

Ghatotkacha's eyes held a flicker of sorrow. "Perhaps. Or perhaps only in fire and wind."

The fifth flame swelled, casting long shadows into the trees.

When Barbarik turned again, his father was gone.

The sage bowed. "You may now carry your arrows unwrapped. The forest has seen what lies within you."

Barbarik did not reply. He simply reached over his shoulder and untied the cloth binding his three arrows. Their metal tips caught the firelight, gleaming like things that remembered the stars.

He walked out of the clearing, past the five fires, toward the edge of the forest.

He was no longer the same boy who had entered.

And the flames did not burn behind him.

They waited.

35

CHAPTER XI

The Hermit and the King

The forests thinned. The soil grew stonier, paths clearer. The air no longer whispered secrets; it merely carried the heat of the northern sun. Barbarik walked with the quiet strength of one who had seen fire and not flinched. Neelashalya hung lightly across his back, as though it had accepted him now. The three arrows, unwrapped and gleaming, caught the breeze but made no sound.

It was nearing dusk when he heard the bells.

Not temple bells. War bells.

They came from the east, near the banks of the river Hiranyavati. Barbarik turned instinctively, his ears trained more by silence than by noise. He climbed a small ridge and peered down.

A caravan was passing a royal one, judging by the golden canopies and the formation of soldiers surrounding it. Flags bearing the sigil of Hastinapura fluttered in the wind: a white elephant on a field of crimson.

At its centre rode a man on a silver chariot. He was older than Barbarik, perhaps in his thirties, with a lean face and calm eyes that took in every movement around him. He was dressed not in ornaments but in armour softened by time and dust. This was no mere prince.

Barbarik descended.

The guards saw him and raised spears.

"Halt!" one barked. "State your name and allegiance!"

Barbarik did not reach for his weapon. He raised an empty hand. "I carry no allegiance yet. Only questions."

The prince stepped down from the chariot himself. "Let him speak," he said.

Barbarik bowed. "I am Barbarik, son of Ghatotkacha. I come from the forests beyond the Vindhyas. I seek to know the world I must one day serve or stand against."

36

The prince regarded him a moment, then smiled faintly. "Then fate is kind. I am Yudhishthira, son of Dharma. Crown prince of Hastinapura, and seeker of truth, though I find less of it than I would wish."

Barbarik inclined his head. "Your name is known, even in forests."

They walked together for a time, the soldiers uneasy but respectful.

Yudhishthira asked him no direct questions, yet his gaze was the kind that revealed more than it probed. "You carry a Rakshasa's bearing," he said at last. "And a kshatriya's calm. That is a rare union."

"I was taught to bear both," Barbarik said.

The prince paused. "May I ask something without offence?"

"You may ask."

"Why three arrows?"

Barbarik hesitated. "Because three is enough."

"For what?"

"To decide a war."

Yudhishthira said nothing for a long time. Then he smiled. "You speak as one who has seen battle. But your eyes are still young."

"They will not stay that way."

Yudhishthira nodded slowly. "Come. Eat with us tonight. There is a hermit I am to meet at a shrine nearby. Perhaps his counsel will serve us both."

They traveled a short way to a small hillock crowned by an ancient fig tree. Beneath it sat a hermit so thin he seemed woven from roots and skin. His eyes were shut, but he opened them as they approached as if he had been waiting for this moment all his life.

"Two dharmas walk toward me," he said. "One known. One waiting to be named."

Yudhishthira folded his hands. "Blessings, Rishi."

Barbarik did the same, though he felt the hermit's gaze pierce deeper than bone.

"You carry a weapon forged not just in metal but in silence," the hermit said to him. "And a burden that is not yet fully yours."

Barbarik sat. "What is it I carry?"

The hermit closed his eyes and let the question settle. The wind stirred the leaves overhead like a thousand whispered mantras.

"You carry choice," he said at last. "The heaviest of all weapons. Stronger than any bow, more dangerous than any sword."

Barbarik's fingers brushed the arrowheads beside him. "I did not choose to be born into this war."

"No," said the hermit. "But you will choose how it ends."

Yudhishthira's eyes flicked toward the younger warrior. He said nothing.

The hermit turned to the prince. "You, too, must choose. Between justice and victory. Between the law and the soul. You both carry different fires, but you will both come to the same battlefield."

He looked up at the sky. "And the world will hold its breath when you do."

Night fell slowly, as if it, too, wished to delay what was coming. The hermit fell into silence again, already gone from the world of men.

Barbarik stood. "I must go."

"Where?" Yudhishthira asked.

"To find what lies at the heart of dharma. Before I stand in its name."

Yudhishthira placed a hand on his shoulder. "Then may your steps remain true, Barbarik of the Three Arrows. May we meet again before the battlefield decides who we are."

Barbarik walked into the darkness without fear. The stars watched him pass.

And somewhere deep in the forest, the fire still remembered his name.

CHAPTER XII

The Arrow of the Future

The riverbed shimmered like hammered silver beneath the unforgiving sun, its banks dry and cracked like the palms of a forgotten god. Barbarik knelt at the water's edge, where a shallow spring still murmured beneath scattered reeds. He dipped his hands into the cool flow, washing the ochre dust of many roads from his skin. The reflection that blinked back at him from the ripples was both familiar and foreign. A boy once shaped by forest winds, now chiseled by distance, burden, and silence.

His face was leaner, his gaze older than his years. The shoulders that once bore a hunter's sling now carried the weight of a bow carved for legends, Neelashalya, resting beside him like a coiled panther, its polished limbs dark as monsoon bark, strung with silver fibre sinew that hummed softly in the heat. The three arrows, wrapped in layers of saffron cloth and sealed in deer-hide, were with him, as always. Though bound, they pulsed with dormant thunder, as though sensing the nearness of what was to come.

He had wandered far from the cradle of his youth. Through dense woods where trees whispered of old wars. Across ravines echoing with wolf-song. Through hamlets trembling at rumours of gathering armies, and cities choking on the weight of too many ambitions. He had tasted the ache of loneliness, the hollowness of injustice, and the strange clarity that only comes to one who walks with no banner but his own conscience.

Yet one truth remained elusive.

They called him the Seer of Avantipura - a sage who had dreamt the end of the Yuga in flashes of flame and frost. Some claimed he had gone blind from the things he'd seen. Others said he spoke now only in riddles, touched by time itself. But none denied that those who found him did not return unchanged.

Barbarik walked northeastward, into lands where the banyan roots curled like fingers over forgotten stone. There, the forest fell unnaturally quiet. No birds called. The wind itself seemed to listen.

As twilight bled across the sky, he came upon a clearing. A still pond lay at its centre, cupped in stone, fed by an underground spring that whispered as it rose. The water's surface was undisturbed, like a mirror held between breaths. At its edge sat the Seer, bare-chested, skin folded like parchment, eyes closed but not asleep. His hair was silver, falling like river mist over his shoulders. A garland of Rudraksha beads circled his neck like a crown of quietness.

As Barbarik approached, the Seer opened his eyes. They were pale, not blind, but lit from within, like coals seen through ash.

"You have come far," he said, voice deep and mossed with time.

Barbarik bowed. "I seek to understand what I carry."

The Seer nodded slowly. "The three that are one. The arrows that do not belong to this age."

Barbarik knelt, and with reverent fingers unwrapped the saffron cloth. The light dimmed around them as if even the forest dared not interrupt. The first arrow shimmered, bright as dawn breaking over a battlefield. The second glowed with a blue-white pulse, like the eye of a gathering storm. The third was harder to see, a shadow wrapped in stillness, but its presence pressed upon the air like fate about to speak.

"They are not weapons" said the Seer. "They are questions."

Barbarik's brow furrowed. "Questions?"

The Seer gestured to the first arrow. "This is Sankalpa, the arrow of intention. It flies to whatever you will it to. And it never misses. It embodies your clarity."

He moved his hand to the second. "This is Pratikriya, the arrow of consequence. It returns always, but what it brings back depends on the choices you made when you sent it. It teaches you what your will has wrought."

And then to the third. "And this is Anagata, the arrow of the future. It strikes only once. And none, not even you, can know what it shall undo or create. It is not bound by your desire, nor your fear. It answers a question that is not yet formed."

Barbarik's voice was barely a whisper. "Then how can I ever use it?"

The Seer's expression did not change. "Because one day, you must. Not to win. Not to destroy. But to preserve something you have not yet understood. It will be when all paths seem equally shadowed, when truth hides behind every lie. In that moment, you must trust not your aim, but your heart."

He rose, limbs moving with the ease of wind over tall grass. "The war is already beginning. Not on fields, but in the minds of men. Dharma and adharma are no longer opposites. They wear each other's faces. When the conches sound, every warrior will think himself just. Every death will believe itself worthy."

Barbarik looked up, eyes dark with unshed knowing. "Tell me, Seer, if I fight, I will change the war. But if I only watch, I betray my blood. Which path brings less harm?"

The Seer looked at him, not with sorrow, but a fierce reverence.

"That," he said, "is the question only your head can answer."

Barbarik shivered. Not from cold, but from a recognition he could not yet name. He wrapped the arrows again, feeling their breath against his skin. Then he bowed deeply, and without another word, turned to leave.

Behind him, the Seer returned to his stillness.

Above, the stars emerged, blinking one by one into being. Their light fell gently over the path ahead, quiet and endless.

And inside the satchel, the third arrow Anagata, stirred. Not with hunger, but with readiness. Like the silence before the name of fate is spoken aloud.

CHAPTER XIII

The Wind Before the Storm

The first dust of war did not rise from Kurukshetra.

It began far earlier, in the silences between conversations, in the way caravan drivers paused at dusk and looked eastward without knowing why. It stirred in temple courtyards where fire altars smoked uncertainly, and in dreams that scattered like startled birds. In these dreams, kings drowned in molten gold, mothers wept without cause, and stars blinked out before their time.

Even the crows, those unasked messengers of the in-between, seemed to carry more than hunger in their cries.

Barbarik had reached the outer plains of Kuru territory, where the land opened wide like a wound. The earth here bore the stamp of abandonment: fields once ripe now lay flat and untended; oxen stood tethered but idle, their eyes dulled by waiting. Trees whispered dry secrets to one another, leaves twitching though the sky held no wind.

But there was wind. It was not the playful teasing of spring nor the guttural surge of monsoon. This was something else, raw, unsettled. It circled the edges of the world like a wolf scenting blood.

Barbarik stood atop a low ridge, gazing out across the land. The horizon shimmered with pale lines of dust, armies on the move, banners unfurling like tongues of fire. From this height, the valley below seemed not like a battlefield, but like a stage being set for something no one could yet name.

Neelashalya hung across his back, silent. The deer-hide satchel at his hip pulsed with quiet weight, three arrows that hummed with unborn decisions. His shadow stretched behind him, long and still.

Below, tucked beside a tree-worn shrine to Gauri, two village women knelt before flickering lamps. The elder wore a deep red sari that clung to her frame like old fire; the younger's hands trembled slightly as she offered marigold petals. Their prayers were half-whispers, but their eyes kept flicking northward.

The elder woman looked up at Barbarik. She did not flinch.

"You are not of these lands," she said simply.

"I go where others fear to go," Barbarik replied.

"Toward the war, then."

He inclined his head.

She rose slowly, approached him, and without hesitation, reached into a cloth pouch. From it, she drew a slender white thread, knotted thrice. With practiced hands, she tied it around his wrist. Her fingers were warm and calloused.

"For vision," she said. "For memory. And for protection. If the gods still grant such things."

Barbarik looked down at the thread. It felt like a quiet promise.

"Thank you."

As he turned to leave, a voice dry as drum-skin, rose from the road below.

"You walk like one who listens for thunder."

He turned. A camel approached, led by a tall figure in weather-worn black robes. A water gourd hung from his waist, a satchel across his back. His beard was shot with grey, and his eyes sparkled like a man who had seen both miracles and executions.

"I am Yatin." he said, dismounting. "Chronicler of things no one wishes to remember."

"A bard?" Barbarik asked.

"A liar," Yatin replied cheerfully, "but one with unusually good recall."

Barbarik allowed himself a rare smile. "And what do you seek?"

"Stories that should not be forgotten. Or perhaps stories better left buried."

They walked together for some time, the camel trailing behind, indifferent to prophecy or doom. The land around them grew increasingly sparse; no birds, no oxen, no children laughing at the roadside. Only the wind, and the faint scent of iron curling through the air.

"You've heard what's coming, I suppose," Yatin said. "Pandavas and Kauravas drawn up like storm clouds. Krishna rides with a whip instead of a flute. Bhishma leads the phalanx. Drona sharpens his silence. And Karna he's the sun's fury given flesh."

Barbarik nodded. "I know."

"And where do you stand?"

"I carry arrows that do not miss. I stand where choice begins."

Yatin paused mid-step.

"Then you're not just a warrior," he said. "You're a threshold."

They stopped at a fork in the road. The setting sun cast the land in hues of burnished gold and deep bronze. The air was heavy with ash, though nothing had yet burned.

"I go south, toward words," Yatin said. "You go east, toward deeds."

Barbarik inclined his head. "May your ink never dry."

"And may your arrows never need to be loosed," Yatin responded.

As the bard disappeared down the slope, Barbarik turned toward Kurukshetra.

From a distance, the great camp looked like a city being born and dying all at once. Silk banners flapped above high poles. Chariots groaned. Horses reared and were soothed. Priests chanted to gods whose ears had grown tired. The clang of steel rang like broken music. Fires were being lit, not for warmth or prayer, but for war.

Barbarik stood at the threshold.

Above, a black hawk spiralled high into the saffron sky. It caught a current that had no name, its wings taut and silent.

Below, the land held its breath.

And through it all walked a youth from the forest, carrying three arrows and a question that the world was not yet ready to answer.

CHAPTER XIV

The Council of Shadows

The royal tents of the Pandava host sprawled across the Kurukshetra plains like a crimson mirage, rippling, breathing, shifting with the restless wind. They were stitched from silken canopies dyed in royal reds and deep golds, anchored by pillars carved from sandalwood and wrapped in prayer-cloths. The fabrics swayed like sails not of ships, but of omens. The great camp did not yet carry the stench of blood, nor the weight of fallen names; it was still a waiting place, a crucible of stillness before the first flame.

Here, amid half-built boundaries of war, fates sharpened themselves not on swords but on silence.

Barbarik stepped into the camp like a shadow stepping into its own source.

He was neither stopped nor hailed. No soldier barred his path, though dozens watched. Some lowered their weapons subtly; others whispered behind armoured hands. It was not fear that stilled them, nor respect. It was something older, a recognition that defied lineage, attire, or the trappings of mortal roles. The bow he bore was carved from storm-wood and breathed faintly of rain. The satchel at his side pulsed with an unseen rhythm, as if it carried not arrows, but time itself bound in threes.

He walked softly, yet with a weight that made the air hold its breath.

The camp was vast. Bannered paths led past rows of war chariots, racks of spears and swords, and fires where armorers hammered breastplates by moonlight. Priests walked barefoot, their foreheads streaked with ash. Horses neighed restlessly, sensing the edge of something greater than battle. War had not yet begun, but the soil already remembered its future.

At the heart of it all stood the Sabha-tent, vast as a king's court but without a throne. Its walls were thick, layered with wool and lined with dyed silk from Kashi and Avanti. Torches burned at each corner, their flames unmoving. This was the council-space, the place where the minds of dharma's chosen gathered, not to speak of glory, but of necessity.

Barbarik entered.

The air within was dense, still. It smelled of incense, sandalwood, and sweat held in tension. The kings and commanders of the Pandava alliance sat on low cushions arranged in a circle, no one above, no one below. Yet even in this circle, the centre held.

Yudhishthira sat with his palms joined, spine straight, his expression carved from restraint and weary dharma. Bhima, broad as a thundercloud, leaned upon his mace like a farmer resting on a plough, yet his gaze never rested. Arjuna, darker of skin and sharper of gaze, sat taut like a drawn bow, each breath measured, each word held behind his teeth. Nakula and Sahadeva flanked them, composed and unreadable, the quiet sentinels of a shared burden.

And near them, in stillness more potent than noise, sat Krishna.

He did not sit at the head, nor speak as a king. But his presence shaped the space around him. Where he looked, silence bent. He had said little since arriving; not out of hesitation, but because he had already begun listening to what others had not yet spoken.

The moment Barbarik stepped across the threshold, the air shifted.

Heads turned. Bhima's eyes narrowed, his hand moving subtly toward his weapon. Arjuna's fingers twitched near the Gandiva. Even Krishna, who had watched storms without blinking, tilted his head slightly, as though measuring the arrival of an unexpected wind.

"I come not to join," Barbarik said, his voice steady as river stone, "but to bear witness."

The silence did not break. It deepened.

Yudhishthira rose with slow dignity. His face glimmered with recognition. "You are the one they call the bearer of the three arrows."

Barbarik bowed lightly. "I am he."

Arjuna's voice followed, cool as the steel he wore. "Then choose a side, stranger. The time for watching is past."

Barbarik's gaze shifted. He did not look at Arjuna. He looked at Krishna.

"And if I choose?" he asked.

Krishna's smile was neither warm nor cold. It was the kind of smile that had watched entire yugas fade into dust. "Then dharma will wear one more mask."

A whisper moved through the tent. Not from lips, but from hearts.

Outside, the wind tugged at the seams of the pavilion like a child eager to open what it did not understand.

Barbarik stepped forward. His voice carried, though it did not rise.

"If I fight, I will fight for dharma. But not as it is claimed by banners or spoken by kings. Not by oath nor by blood. I will fight for the truth that remains after the last lie falls silent."

Bhima scoffed, his voice a snort of disbelief. "And who are you to decide such truth?"

Before another breath could be drawn, Krishna raised his hand.

"You speak with fire, son of the wind," he said, his voice gentle and unhurried. "But fire does not ask why it burns."

Bhima lowered his eyes.

Barbarik looked around; not at the men, but at the spaces between them. The space where old pain sat coiled like a serpent. The space where oaths weighed heavier than chariots. The space where unspoken ambition hung like a sword over every head.

He saw not a council, but a storm. Not warriors, but waves already breaking. He saw Kurukshetra not as a war yet to begin, but as a fate already chosen.

Krishna broke the silence again.

"Will you fight in this war?"

Barbarik placed a hand on his satchel, where three arrows slept, dreaming of conclusions. His eyes were calm. They held neither certainty nor fear, only the burden of one who sees too clearly.

"Only when I understand," he said. "Only when I see."

Krishna nodded. "Then see. Stay. Watch."

No more words were offered. No more were needed.

Barbarik turned and walked out of the tent, his footsteps as silent as they had entered. Behind him, the council remained still, as if a gust had passed but not left.

That evening, Barbarik did not return to the pavilions nor seek rest among warriors. He found a pipal tree at the edge of the camp, where the torches flickered faintly and the sky began its descent into stars. He sat beneath its broad, whispering leaves, arms resting across his knees.

The sun dipped behind thorny ridges, dyeing the sky in shades of rust and sorrow. Campfires flickered across the plain like tiny prayers cast into darkness. Drums began to speak, slow, deliberate beats like heartbeats counting down to destiny.

Above, the first star emerged, pale and watchful.

And somewhere beyond the reach of sight or sound, something ancient stirred. A presence older than gods, older than questions, older even than names. It stirred like a wheel long stilled, preparing once again to turn.

Barbarik closed his eyes, listening.

The silence was no longer empty.

It was full of the weight of all things to come.

CHAPTER XV

When the Father Returns

The forest beyond the Pandava camp was no longer merely a haven of trees and birdsong. It had become a place with breath. A listening place. A place that remembered.

Its mood had turned from somnolent to expectant, though it showed no outward sign. The banyans still draped their serpent roots into the loam, and the neem trees still stood in crooked congregation. Yet there was something in the way the leaves rustled now, not with the idle gossip of wind but with intent, as if whispering secrets to those who dared hear. The air had grown thick with the scent of sap and still rain. Every step Barbarik took sank slightly deeper into the earth, as though the land itself was reluctant to let him go.

He walked here often.

Since Krishna had asked him to remain a witness, he had roamed not just the camps but the woods beyond, places where silence grew tall and unbroken. His eyes had learned to watch the patterns of men, but his heart had learned to listen elsewhere; to the flicker of fireflies that blinked out at certain names, to the sudden hush in birdsong when thoughts of war brushed the trees, and to his own heartbeat, which thudded now not with restlessness but with an ever-deepening weight.

It was on such an evening, beneath a bruised sky swollen with the promise of storm, that his feet found once more the clearing that lived in his bones more than in memory.

He did not need to be guided. The path unfolded beneath him like an old lullaby, remembered by muscle, not mind. There were the neem trees again, gnarled and twisted like the fingers of time. There lay the stones, toothy and moss-covered, guardians who neither questioned nor yielded. The undergrowth thinned where the moonlight fell, a pale pool of silver milk on the forest floor.

And there, in the heart of it, as though carved from the dusk itself, stood Ghatotkacha.

This time, there was no surprise between them.

"I wondered if you would come again," Barbarik said, stepping into the clearing.

"I never left," Ghatotkacha replied, his voice a slow thunder rolling after distant lightning.

He stood motionless, tall as twilight, his silhouette outlined by the quicksilver sheen of moonlight breaking through the branches. The colour of his skin had not changed; still the deep grey of monsoon clouds before a downpour, but his presence had softened. Where once he had stood like a storm barely held at bay, now he felt more like a river nearing its estuary, powerful, yes, but tempered by acceptance.

Barbarik came closer. The grass parted with reverence, whispering with every step.

"You walk the edge of two worlds," the son said, his voice calm but weighted with awe.

Ghatotkacha nodded once, slow and deliberate. "The forest allows me passage. And the wind listens to blood."

They stood a breath apart, but between them stretched years unshared. A stillness gathered around them, not awkward, not forced, but whole. As if the trees themselves held their breath.

"I thought you had returned to the north," Barbarik said after a pause, scanning the great form that was at once familiar and strange.

"I did," Ghatotkacha murmured, his eyes distant. "But the war calls louder now. And not just to the living."

Barbarik knelt, placing his palm against the earth. "This place remembers."

Ghatotkacha's expression darkened, the memory of countless battles flickering behind his eyes. "Soon, I will be summoned. Not by name, but by need. I will rise because dharma will demand a blood offering. And when that hour comes, you must not mourn me."

Barbarik looked up, face bare of emotion but heavy with feeling. "I have never known you long enough to mourn. But I will carry you."

The forest stirred as if moved by that vow. Somewhere, an owl hooted, once, twice, then fell silent.

The Rakshasa stepped forward. From his belt, he withdrew a small shard of bone; not jagged, but smooth, as if time had polished it. A spiral mark had been etched into it, not written, but sung into form. He placed it gently in Barbarik's palm.

"Your grandfather gave me this when I was a boy," he said. "It's from the spine of a Vanara chieftain who fought beside Rama. They say it does not break."

Barbarik studied it. The talisman was warm, almost pulsing. He could feel it, not just its shape, but its story. The weight of a thousand yesterdays. His fingers curled around it like roots seeking earth.

"It's not for battle," Ghatotkacha added softly. "It's for memory."

"I will keep it," Barbarik said.

"I know," his father replied.

A silence passed. But it was not empty. It brimmed with all the words that had never been said; lullabies unheard, tales unshared, wounds untended. And still, it did not ache. It simply was.

"You've grown," the father said at last.

"So have you," the son replied.

They both smiled. It was not wide, but it was real.

For a fleeting moment; brief as breath, eternal as bond, they stood as father and son. Not as prince and rakshasa, not as warrior and wraith. Just two lives caught in the great weaving of fate.

Ghatotkacha turned then, already dissolving into half-shadow, half-memory. The forest parted to let him go.

But just before he vanished entirely into the mist-heavy thickets, he paused.

"Barbarik," he said, not turning. "When the war begins, you will see truths that shame the sky. Do not let them steal your flame."

Barbarik's voice followed him, steady but quiet. And if I must choose?"

Ghatotkacha's reply came like the echo of dew falling, soft, certain, and irreversible.

"Then choose as the forest does, by what survives after fire."

And he was gone.

Barbarik stood alone.

But not lonely.

His hand closed around the bone talisman. The other rested lightly on the shaft of Neelashalya.

In his quiver, the arrow stirred once, not in hunger, but in recognition.

Above him, the sky exhaled. The first raindrops fell, not harsh but cool, like blessings. The forest, it seemed, had heard. And approved.

Somewhere far off, the war drums began again.

But Barbarik stayed awhile longer, between the last light and the first thunder, between memory and foretelling.

For now, that was enough.

CHAPTER XVI

Threads of Dharma

The air had changed.

Not in temperature or wind or scent alone, but in the way silence held its breath. It was as though the very fabric of time had been stretched thin across the battlefield, taut like a bowstring drawn to its furthest limit, quivering before the release. Everything; every movement, every decision, every word, now carried the gravity of inevitability.

Each dawn arrived not with birdsong, but with the brazen cry of conch shells, echoing over the plain like the voice of fate itself. Drums followed, their cadence pulsing like the heartbeat of the gathering war. And when night fell, it brought no peace. Only murmurings of dreams troubled, of gods displeased, of omens spotted in fire and entrails and flight of birds.

Barbarik watched it all.

And waited.

Krishna had spoken little to him since that first encounter by the river. Yet Barbarik saw him often, gliding across the camp with a quietness that belied his centrality to everything unfolding. Krishna was everywhere and nowhere, appearing beside Yudhishthira during grave councils, whispering to Arjuna in the shade of the war chariot, laughing too easily with Draupadi as if laughter itself were a blade that dulled fear. Sometimes, Barbarik glimpsed him at the river's edge long after midnight, gazing into the water as if listening for something only he could hear.

Barbarik was beginning to understand.

He had come expecting fire. Steel. Fury unleashed like a summer storm.

But what he found was more intricate.

War, he was learning, was not simply fought. It was woven, thread by thread, through strategy and silence, through ambition disguised as duty, and duty muddied by pain. Beneath every polished command lay unspoken truths. In every warrior's stride was a shadow of doubt.

One afternoon, Barbarik stood on the periphery of a gathering. The war council was underway.

At its heart sat Yudhishthira, robes creased and eyes sunken with the weight of choices no righteous man wished to make. Beside him, Bhima loomed, still and immense, his arms folded like a siege waiting for release. Arjuna, face unreadable, fingers tapping lightly on the hilt of Gandiva, sat poised like an arrow held in breath. Nakula and Sahadeva flanked them, eyes alert, expressions solemn.

And Krishna.

Krishna did not speak first. He never did.

But when he did, it was as though the wind leaned in. Barbarik could not catch the exact words, but he saw their ripples: Yudhishthira's trembling nod, Bhima's jaw set tighter than his mace grip, a flicker, quick as a darting bird, of apprehension in Sahadeva's gaze. Even Arjuna, ever composed, drew a slow breath.

When the council dispersed, the men walked past him like stones sliding off a mountain, heavy with unspoken things.

Barbarik turned to go.

But Krishna's voice caught him. Quiet. Intent.

"Walk with me."

They left the canvas tents behind. The grass grew taller here. The earth felt looser underfoot, as though it remembered no banner, no blood. They passed groves where trees grew older, thicker. The canopy above filtered the sun into a thousand shifting coins of light.

Krishna walked with the ease of one who carries the burden of worlds without bending.

"You've been watching," he said.

Barbarik nodded. "As you asked me to."

"And what have you seen?"

Barbarik looked ahead, voice calm. "Not war. Not yet. Only its shape. A shape made by men who believe they serve dharma, but more often serve only the ghosts of their grief."

Krishna stopped beside a blooming kadamba tree. The blossoms had unfurled early, tiny yellow stars trembling against the wind, defying season and logic.

"Do you know," Krishna asked softly, "why this war cannot be avoided?"

Barbarik thought for a moment. "Because no one truly wishes to stop it."

Krishna's eyes darkened. Not in anger, but in knowledge so vast it could not be carried with joy. "Yes," he said. "Each man believes himself wronged. Each wears dharma like armour. But inside, there is fire. And pride. The war is not born of justice. It is born of wounds."

Barbarik's brow furrowed. "Then why am I here, Krishna? If dharma is a veil for vengeance, why must I be its judge?"

Krishna turned to face him. A breeze stirred the edge of his yellow robe; the sunlight caught in his hair like threads of gold unspooling.

"You are here," he said, "because you see. Not with ambition. Not with legacy. But with stillness. You were raised outside the noise of courts and curses. You have strength, but more than that, you have clarity."

Barbarik was silent. One hand rested on the curve of Neelashalya, the other loosely at his side.

"Do you know," Krishna continued, "what makes your arrows terrifying?"

"Their vow," Barbarik answered quietly. "That once loosed, they do not return unspent. That they seek the end of all that stands."

Krishna nodded. "And that is why you cannot fight."

Barbarik's eyes snapped to him. "What do you mean?"

"If you entered this war," Krishna said, "it would be over before it began. You would strike once, and the field would fall silent. No struggle. No questioning. No unraveling of truths. You would erase the war, and with it, the lesson."

Barbarik's voice was low, steady. "So even this; carnage, betrayal, the slaughter of kin, it has purpose?"

Krishna's expression was unreadable. "Even poison can be medicine. And even gods must let the wheel turn. Karma must be lived, not bypassed."

The forest around them held still. A peacock called in the distance, shrill and lonely.

Krishna reached out and placed a hand on Barbarik's shoulder. "Your time will come. Not to strike. But to witness. And when that hour comes, you must be like the fire, clear and consuming. But you must also be like the ash, soft, accepting, without pride. Can you be both?"

Barbarik lowered his gaze. "I do not like it," he said. "But I understand."

Krishna smiled then. Not in triumph, not even in comfort, but as one who sees a storm and still walks into it.

"That is enough. For now."

They stood beneath the kadamba tree, its blossoms gently falling around them like offerings. Behind them, the camp stirred. The chants of priests rose like smoke, twining with the clang of whetstones on blade. Prayer and violence braided into a single river, flowing toward an unseen shore.

And Barbarik, son of the wind and the unseen mountain, stood still.

He had come to end a war.

Now, he was learning why he must watch it begin.

CHAPTER XVII

The War Begins

Dawn bled across the plains of Kurukshetra, a slow unfurling of blood-orange fire on the eastern edge of the sky. The land seemed to hold its breath, not a leaf stirred, not a bird called. The air itself felt suspended, as though the earth had become aware of what was about to transpire and was bracing for the first wound.

Across the vast horizon, the two armies stood poised; immense, unmoving, mirror reflections of rage and righteousness. On one side, the black and crimson banners of Hastinapura hung like war-wounds against the wind, emblazoned with the sigils of serpents, suns, and snarling beasts. Rows upon rows of Kaurava soldiers bristled with iron, their armour glinting dully in the bruised light. On the opposite flank, the Pandava forces gleamed, white banners streaked with blue, golden chariots harnessed to snorting steeds, and the crests of dharma raised high as if justice itself had taken form.

Barbarik stood alone on the rise of a gentle hill, just beyond the reach of either army's shadow. A solitary figure beneath an ancient pipal tree, he bore witness to the world balanced on the cusp of cataclysm. He had remained here, as Krishna had asked; close enough to see, distant enough not to act. His bow, Neelashalya, rested cool against his back, silent yet aware, like a serpent waiting to stir. His quiver, heavy with the burden of unspent vows, thrummed faintly, arrows that could end all this before it began, if loosed.

But he did not move. He watched.

And what he saw now was not glory. It was gravity. It was inevitability.

The first sound came from the heart of the Kaurava ranks; a slow, thunderous drumbeat, like the heartbeat of the earth itself awakening. The response came sharp and piercing, conches from the Pandava lines, high and cold like the cry of a hawk before the dive. The sky seemed to darken for a breath.

Then it began.

The banners surged. Chariots creaked into motion. Shields locked with ringing finality. Thousands of feet began to march in rhythm, the sound of men moving toward destiny, toward death, toward legend.

Kurukshetra had awakened.

Barbarik's gaze did not waver, but his heart did. It clenched. Not with fear, but with something deeper, sorrow laced with clarity.

Behind him, soft footsteps whispered through the grass. He turned.

It was a boy.

No older than ten, barefoot, thin as a reed, with a dhoti too large for his frame and streaks of ash on his cheeks. His eyes, dark and wide, carried something older than his years.

"You're the one they call Shyam, the tri-baan dhaari." the boy said, voice unsteady.

Barbarik tilted his head slightly. "Some do."

"They say your arrows never miss."

"They say many things."

The boy's gaze turned to the battlefield, now alive with sound and dust and motion. "My brother is down there," he murmured. "He joined Duryodhana's men. He said it was for food. But my mother says this war is not about food."

Barbarik knelt, folding his limbs slowly, his eyes level with the child's. The wind stirred the edge of his black garments.

"What do you think it's about?? he asked softly.

The boy frowned, biting his lip. "I think, it's about people forgetting how to listen."

Barbarik's face broke into a brief smile. "You're not wrong."

The child reached into a small pouch tied to his waist and pulled out a seed, small, brown, ordinary in appearance.

"My mother says we have to plant these when the war is over. Even if it takes a hundred years before they grow."

He placed the seed in Barbarik's outstretched palm; a fragile thing, easily lost in the wind. Yet somehow, in that moment, it felt heavier than any weapon Barbarik had ever carried.

He closed his fingers around it, cradling it like it was the last memory of peace.

The boy turned and slipped away into the trees, vanishing like a spirit unclaimed by the battlefield.

Below, the sound of war surged, not as a single roar but a thousand separate screams woven into one. The thunder of hooves, the crash of metal upon metal, the cry of names called into a sky already filled with the weight of ancestral blood.

And then Barbarik saw him.

His father.

Ghatotkacha.

No longer the silent giant of the forest, no longer the laughing shadow beneath moonlight - now a titan of wrath, a cyclone made flesh. He rose from the Pandava lines like a storm given form, clad in war-iron, crowned with braids that coiled like living ropes, arms like tree trunks swinging a mace that shattered chariots in a single blow. His laughter cracked across the field like lightning, wild, feral, chilling.

Rakshasas screamed in exultation behind him. Enemy ranks broke before his onslaught. Horses reared and bolted. Men scattered like dust before the wind.

But Barbarik's heart did not swell.

It broke.

He understood now what Krishna had meant. Every hero here was not just a warrior, but a thread in a cosmic loom, tugged, twisted, sacrificed. None of them were untouched. Not Arjuna. Not Bhishma. Not Ghatotkacha.

And certainly not himself.

The air shifted. A breeze moved across the hill, scented faintly with lotus, ash, and something harder to name. A memory, perhaps, of something holy yet forgotten.

Barbarik turned.

Krishna was beside him.

No footfall had marked his coming. He simply was, as if the wind had shaped itself into a man, as if the battlefield itself had called for a witness and he had arrived.

He said nothing for a long time.

They stood together, eyes on the chaos below, fire and flesh, wheel and wing, blood and prayer. Krishna's face was still, unreadable, not with indifference but with something deeper, the weight of knowing, the stillness that comes when time itself pauses to see what choice will be made.

Barbarik opened his hand, revealing the seed.

"A child gave me this," he said.

Krishna's gaze did not leave the field. But his voice was gentle.

"Even in war, life remembers how to begin again."

Barbarik closed his fingers, enclosing the seed once more.

"But what if nothing survives?" he asked.

Krishna turned to him, and for a moment, the sky seemed to deepen behind his eyes, not blue, but black and infinite, like the space between stars.

"Then you must."

The words fell into the silence like stones into a still pond, rippling outward, quiet but irreversible.

Below, the war raged on. Wheels crushed bone. Fire kissed banners. Names of gods and ancestors were invoked with the desperation of dying men.

But atop the hill, Barbarik stood still.

He understood now.

He was not here to strike.

Not yet.

He was here to see.

To remember.

To carry this truth; terrible, sacred, and unfiltered, not in legend, not in song, but in silence, in witnessing. Until the world was ready to listen again.

And perhaps, when it did, someone would still be alive to plant what had once been given, a seed, small and brown, held against the storm.

CHAPTER XVIII

The Head That Watches

The battlefield trembled beneath the weight of fate.

Above it all, the sun burned a deeper gold, as though reluctant to rise over what it knew must come. The winds that once whispered through the trees now circled in silence, holding their breath. Across Kurukshetra, the war had become a tide, roaring, relentless, inevitable. Horses screamed, chariot wheels split the earth, and the cries of dying men rose like ash. But amid it all, Barbarik heard none of it.

He stood beneath the pipal tree, where the seed of life rested in his palm, quiet, weightless, infinite. Its stillness was heavier than the chaos around him, heavier than even the sword he had once swung with pride.

Beside him, Krishna stood barefoot in the grass, serene in a world unraveling. The hem of his peacock-blue angavastram stirred faintly with the breeze, like a river remembering its rhythm. In his presence, the air itself seemed to pause. He was not a charioteer now, nor a messenger. He was the witness of beginnings and ends.

"It is time," the blue-limbed one said softly.

Barbarik did not flinch. His gaze was clear, like water that had seen the bottom of its well.

"I have watched," he said. "I have seen every thread of this tapestry unfold, each arrow loosed, each vow broken, each heart cracked open like fruit in the sun. I know now what the weight of my arrows would be. I know what victory would cost."

Krishna stepped toward him. Not as a god descending, but as a friend arriving.

"You asked for the price of dharma," Barbarik continued. "Here it is."

He removed Neelashalya from his back and laid it at Krishna's feet, the great bow resting like a fallen tree that had outlived the storm. The wind stirred again, slow and reverent.

Krishna looked at the weapon. Then at the man.

"You have walked far to arrive at this moment," he said. "From the red jungles of the north to the trembling edge of the world's great wound. You came as a boy with questions burning behind your eyes. You leave as a man who knows the weight of seeing."

Barbarik knelt. With deliberate hands, he undid the cloth that bound his thick, braided hair. From beneath it, he drew the simple crown his mother had woven long ago, a circlet of copper leaves and forest feathers, faded but unbroken. He placed it beside the bow.

"I offer you my head," he said. "Not as a weapon. But as an eye. So that the world may see not only what war destroys, but what it forgets."

A hush settled over the moment, deep, sacred, older than time. Even the birds in the trees were silent, as though nature itself had turned its gaze to witness.

Krishna knelt beside him. His hand, cool and steady, touched Barbarik's brow.

"May your sight endure beyond flesh," he whispered. "May your voice speak even in stillness. May your gaze remain steady, as truth must be."

He stood slowly. Time bent around him like a bowstring drawn. In one fluid motion, neither swift nor hesitant, he raised his discus. Sudarshana shimmered in his palm, rimmed with light and silence, carved with the memory of stars.

Barbarik closed his eyes.

There was no pain.

Only light.

Then darkness.

Then

Vision.

They placed the head on a high stone, carved smooth by centuries of rain and wind, overlooking all of Kurukshetra. From that height, the field below was not a battlefield, but a map of human reckoning, a great churning sea of karma.

Krishna washed the severed head with water drawn from the Ganga, its chill cutting through the dawn like truth through illusion. The water streamed over the closed eyes, down the cheeks, and pooled at the base of the stone.

Morvi came quietly. Dressed in white, draped in silence. Her hands were gentle, though her eyes had not blinked since she arrived. Without a word, she placed a garland of wildflowers, jasmine, flame lily, and parijat, around the neck. A single tear slid down her cheek but did not fall.

Behind her stood Ghatotkacha, vast as a hill, yet hollowed by sorrow. His great hands trembled at his sides, open yet powerless. His eyes did not leave the face of his son.

A breeze stirred. Krishna leaned forward and whispered a mantra, not in Sanskrit, not in any human tongue, but in the syllables of wind and river, stone and fire. Only the elements heard. Only the gods understood.

And then,

The head opened its eyes.

Not with magic.

But with knowing.

The irises glowed faintly; not golden, nor silver, but a colour that remembered the first dawn. In those eyes were fire and ocean, ruin and renewal. The field below was no longer just a war. It was a parable in flesh.

Barbarik had become what he was meant to be.

Not a warrior of the sword.

But a witness.

A seer of what men forget.

A mirror held up to the faces of kings and sages, showing them not who they believed they were, but what they chose to become.

And the seed remained clutched in his palm, unseen now, yet eternal.

CHAPTER XIX

The Cost of Silence

The earth groaned beneath the weight of war.

Kurukshetra, once a fertile expanse of grassland kissed by the Yamuna's breeze, had become an altar of ruin. The sky hung low, heavy with smoke and fate. Fires danced across the horizon like memories refusing to die, and the wind, once scented with jasmine and til, now carried the iron stench of blood.

But for Barbarik, no longer warrior, no longer son, no longer flesh, none of it stirred breath or blade.

He was but a severed head, nestled upon a slab of dark stone atop a forgotten hill, eyes open and unmoving. Yet within those eyes, the world churned.

He saw not with sight, but with something deeper. Something unshackled.

Kurukshetra sprawled below him, not merely as a battlefield, but as a scripture unfolding. Its verses written not in ink but in agony. Each groan of metal, each scream lost to the wind, etched itself into the eternal memory of earth. It was no longer a war between cousins. It was the reckoning of an age.

From that high vantage, Barbarik bore silent witness.

He saw chariots shattered like hollow promises, their wheels spinning in vain as if the ground itself rejected the burden they carried. He saw spears rise like questions and fall like verdicts. Banners, once proud with clan and creed, now fluttered as ashen rags over corpses who no longer cared for lineage.

The land had lost its colour. Even the sun, a weary sentinel, seemed reluctant to gaze too long upon the carnage.

Beside him stood Krishna.

Unmoving. Eternal.

His form shimmered faintly, not with light, but with the quiet gravity of one who carries time itself in his glance. His gaze swept across the field not with despair, nor with anger, but with a knowing too ancient to name. He did not flinch. He did not grieve. He simply was.

The silence between them stretched wide; wider than any war could cross.

It was not the silence of absence, but of origin. The silence before the first mantra was uttered. Before the first flame licked air. Before truth learned to wear masks.

Down below, Arjuna moved like a poem trapped in a battlefield. His arrows whispered death with surgical grace, yet each kill dimmed the light in his eyes. He, the peerless archer, carved through the enemy line with purpose, but his soul flinched at every cry. The Gandiva sang, but it sang dirges.

Yudhishthira, the just, barked commands torn from the seams of his conscience. Every order was a weight he had never wished to bear. His dharma, once a guiding star, now flickered beneath layers of necessity and regret. The crown upon his brow gleamed, but it pressed down like a curse.

Bhima roared through the field, a storm in flesh. His mace shattered bone and memory alike. Yet each strike, no matter how brutal, left him emptier. Rage was his offering, but peace never came. Even vengeance, Barbarik saw, was a hollow god.

On the other side, valour bled just as bright.

Duryodhana stood defiant, bloodied yet unbowed. He had lost brothers, allies, dreams, but not pride. Pride clung to him like a second skin, whispering of legacy, of the throne he was born to defend. Even as hope thinned, he fought, not for victory, but for meaning.

And Karna?

O radiant, cursed Karna.

Golden no more. His armour stripped by deceit, his birthright denied by fate, his every triumph punished by the gods he still honoured. When his chariot wheel sank into the treacherous soil, he did not cry out. He met death like he had met life; head high, heart bared.

Barbarik watched them all fall.

Not with judgment. Not with pity.

But with the still clarity of one who had relinquished sides.

He saw how righteousness fractured into opinion. How dharma bent beneath the weight of context. How every hero bled red, and every villain prayed before battle.

Good and evil had not perished - they had simply unmasked themselves.

His silence was no longer the silence of obedience. No longer the vow of a son honouring a god's request.

It had become the silence of reckoning. Of realisation.

Krishna's voice, when it came, was quieter than wind stirring ash.

"Do you see it now, Barbarik?"

Barbarik's voice rose like breath from the deep earth, patient and vast.

"I see it all."

Krishna turned, and in his eyes lay a sorrow so complete, even gods could not bear it aloud.

"And what will you do now, my friend?"

Barbarik paused. Not to think, but to feel.

"I will wait," he said. "Until the last of them falls."

The silence that followed did not echo.

It held.

It held the weight of a thousand lifetimes. Of regrets whispered only to the night. Of truths too dangerous for scriptures.

Barbarik had become what he was destined to be.

Not a warrior. Not a conqueror. Not a prince forgotten in the margins.

But the witness.

The gaze that would not blink.

The eye that would remember when memory itself crumbled.

And as the sun dipped low, casting long shadows over the blood-stained earth, Barbarik remained, still, seeing, sacred.

Waiting.

For the war to end.
And for the silence to begin again.

CHAPTER XX

The Weight of a Thousand Silent Witnesses

The sun was beginning to set on the battlefield of Kurukshetra, but the silence that had fallen over the war-torn land was not the peaceful quiet of resolution. It was the silence of a world that had watched its own soul fracture and now waited for the inevitable reckoning.

Barbarik's head, now an eternal witness to the ebb and flow of time, saw the land beyond the battlefield where life would soon begin to heal, but never quite forget the scars of the war. In the distance, the Pandavas, their victory hard-won and yet hollow, prepared to return to Hastinapura. Their bodies were battered, their hearts heavy with the knowledge of all that had been lost.

Krishna stood beside Barbarik's stone, his form distant but his presence all-encompassing. The last of the great warriors had fallen, but the ripples of their choices would last far beyond this day.

"The world changes, Barbarik," Krishna said softly. "And yet, it does not."

Barbarik's gaze remained fixed, seeing the victory that was not truly a victory the Pandavas had triumphed, yes, but at what cost? The brothers had each lost something whether it was their kingdom, their honour, or their own souls. Even Yudhishthira, the righteous king, now burdened with the knowledge of the destruction his decisions had wrought, could not claim true victory.

"You understand now," Krishna continued, his voice carrying the weight of eons. "It is not the battle itself that defines a man. It is the choices he makes within it, the truths he accepts in its aftermath."

Barbarik felt the weight of those words settle deep into his bones. The choices of war, the lies of honour, the betrayal of trust none of it could be undone. His purpose, his existence, was not to participate in the war, but to bear witness to it. He was the mirror that reflected the world's greatest triumphs and its most crushing failures.

As the last of the Kauravas fell, and the earth fell silent, Barbarik's heart stirred. He could not help but feel a pang of sorrow for the world that had been left behind, for the souls of the fallen warriors who had fought in the name of something greater, only to realise too late that they were fighting for something that could never be.

And yet, even in that sorrow, there was a quiet wisdom that settled over him. He had watched the rise of heroes and the fall of kings. He had seen the choices that had led them to this moment their great deeds, their small betrayals, their misunderstandings. And through it all, he had come to understand that the world was not shaped by the grandest of actions, but by the smallest, most hidden choices. The ones that no one ever saw. The ones that remained buried in the hearts of men.

Krishna spoke once more, as though reading Barbarik's mind. "Your head, Barbarik, was never meant to be a weapon. It was meant to be a witness. And now, the story of this war, the story of your existence, will be passed down through the ages, not as a tale of a warrior, but as a tale of silence the silence that saw the world for what it truly was."

Barbarik could feel the weight of those words, and yet, something stirred within him something deeper than the silence he had known all his life. It was the understanding that his journey was not over. His purpose, though fulfilled in its most profound sense, was still part of the ever-turning wheel of fate.

He turned his gaze toward Krishna, the god who had guided him, who had shown him the world in all its splendour and ruin.

"What now, Krishna?" Barbarik asked, his voice a whisper that seemed to echo in the emptiness. "What becomes of the world now that the war is over?"

Krishna smiled faintly, his eyes reflecting the eternal dance of time. "The world will continue, Barbarik. It always does. The Pandavas will return to Hastinapura, but their victory will be tainted by the knowledge that it came at the cost of all that they once held dear. They will rule, but they will rule with the weight of what they have lost."

"And what of me?" Barbarik asked, his heart aching with a sorrow that had no name.

Krishna's smile deepened, but it was tinged with sorrow. "You have seen the truth, Barbarik. Your role is not to shape the world, but to witness it. The stories of heroes and kings will be told for generations, but the true cost of their actions will be remembered only by those who choose to listen by those who choose to see."

As the last light of day disappeared over the horizon, Krishna's voice grew softer, as if carried by the wind itself.

"Your silence will be the last truth spoken. The world will go on. But you, Barbarik, will be the keeper of the silence that carries it forward."

With those words, the earth itself seemed to exhale, as though releasing the breath it had held since the beginning of the war. The weight of history had been recorded, but Barbarik's silence would remain unbroken, eternal.

And in that silence, Barbarik understood.

CHAPTER XXI

The Echoes of a Kingless Throne

It had been days since the last battle cries faded, and the echoes of war began to dissipate into the winds of Kurukshetra. The dust had settled, and the earth, once scarred by the blood of countless warriors, was slowly beginning to heal. The Pandavas had emerged victorious, but their victory was far from celebratory.

Hastinapura was a city caught between the past and the future, a kingdom that had seen glory and ruin. The streets, which had once echoed with the laughter of children and the footsteps of warriors, now stood silent. The people, though they had their king back, had no joy in their hearts. They knew the cost of the throne so many had died, so many families shattered, and no amount of rule could bring back what had been lost.

Barbarik's spirit hovered over the land, his gaze as unyielding as the stone that held his head. He had watched the war unfold from his place in the void, and now, as the aftermath took shape, he saw the truth that no one else could see: the battle had been won, but the war within the hearts of the survivors was far from over.

The Pandavas gathered in the grand hall of Hastinapura, the weight of their rule heavy upon them. The throne, once a symbol of strength and power, now seemed like a hollow thing an empty seat that had cost so much. Yudhishthira, the eldest, sat at the head of the council, his eyes darkened by the burden of kingship. Though he had won the war, his heart was heavy with the knowledge that the bloodshed could never be undone.

"Victory," Yudhishthira's voice broke the silence, but his words were hollow. "What is victory, if it only brings suffering in its wake? What is the use of a throne, if it only reminds us of those we have lost?"

Bhima, his brother, leaned forward, his broad chest heaving with the weight of his own thoughts. He had fought for his family, for his kingdom, but he knew that no amount of strength could fill the emptiness left by the war. "Victory is nothing but a fleeting dream," Bhima said. "It has cost us more than we can ever reclaim."

Arjuna, the great archer, was silent. His bow rested beside him, a reminder of the skill that had led to the destruction of so many. Though he had been a hero on the battlefield, the faces of the fallen haunted him. He had killed with a steady hand, but the price had been steep.

Draupadi, who had borne the brunt of this war's cruelty, stood apart, her eyes distant, lost in thought. She, too, had been shaped by the war, but her scars were different. They were the scars of a woman who had seen her family torn apart, of a queen who had lost not just her honour but her peace.

Barbarik's spirit, still hovering in the silence, felt the weight of their pain. These were not the warriors he had seen before the war, not the people he had known before they had walked the path of bloodshed. The men and women who sat before him were different. They were survivors, but survivors of a war that had broken them in ways they could never fully understand.

"I saw the truth, Krishna," Barbarik whispered to the void, knowing that the God would hear him. "I saw it in the eyes of those who fought. I saw it in their souls. This war this victory it was never meant to be. It was a story we had to tell, but it was not the right story."

Krishna, standing by the door of the hall, his presence calm and knowing, spoke with a voice that echoed through the silence. "Barbarik, your journey has been one of sacrifice. But it is not for you to decide the fate of these souls. The war is over, and it is they who must live with the choices they made."

"But they are not free, Krishna," Barbarik's voice trembled as he spoke. "How can they live with these choices? How can they return to a life they no longer know?"

"They will not return to what they knew," Krishna replied. "For nothing remains as it was. The world will change, as it always does. And so must they."

The words were simple, but they held a weight that settled upon Barbarik's spirit. He had seen it he had seen the way the world bent in response to the choices of the few. The gods may have shaped the course of fate, but it was the lives of mortals that gave it meaning.

In the days that followed, the Pandavas sought to rebuild their kingdom, but it was clear that there would be no easy restoration. The land, though fertile, had been poisoned by the bloodshed. The people, though they had longed for peace, could not forget the violence that had claimed their hearts.

Barbarik's spirit, still bound to his head, gazed upon the remnants of the world he had known. He knew the truth now that no war could ever be truly won, for the scars it left would never heal. But he also knew that the cycle of life would continue. The kingdom would rise again, but it would rise with the knowledge of its own fragility.

As the days turned into weeks, and the weeks into months, Barbarik's presence grew quieter, more distant. He had witnessed the war, and now he watched the slow process of healing, of acceptance. The Pandavas, though they carried the weight of their actions, had a responsibility now to guide the people of Hastinapura. But in their hearts, they knew that they would never fully erase the marks of the war.

And so, with the passing of time, Barbarik's story faded into the background of the world. His sacrifice, his offering, would become a part of the myth a story of a warrior who had given everything, not for victory, but for truth.

The world would move forward. The kingdoms would rise and fall, as they always had. And somewhere, in the deep silence of his stone resting place, Barbarik's head would remain, watching, waiting, as the story of the world continued to unfold.

CHAPTER XXII

The Eternal Witness

The years passed, and the world of Hastinapura, like all kingdoms, rose and fell with time. The Pandavas, having completed their rule, passed the mantle to the next generation, but their legacy tainted by the sacrifices, the choices, and the bloodshed of the war lingered in the hearts of the people.

The land grew quiet again. In the distant fields, where the sounds of battle once rang, only the whispers of the wind remained. The same mountains that had witnessed the fall of great warriors now looked down upon a kingdom recovering from the weight of its past.

But amidst this quiet, one name remained a name that had long since become legend, whispered on the tongues of sages and kings alike. It was the name of Barbarik, the warrior who had offered his life for a cause none but the gods could fully understand. The name of the son who had never known the warmth of his father's embrace, yet had forged a destiny of his own, one that spanned across the realms of mortals and immortals alike.

In the years following the great war, a temple was built at the edge of Kurukshetra, at the very site where Barbarik had once stood headless, yet whole. The stone altar, untouched by time, was inscribed with the words:

He who offered all, yet asked for nothing.

He who stood witness to the fall of empires, but never swayed.

The Khatu Shyam temple became a place of pilgrimage, where kings and commoners alike came to pay their respects, to seek the wisdom of a warrior who had known both the deepest sorrows and the highest truths.

It was said that, though Barbarik had no body, his spirit walked the earth still, watching over the lands he had loved. There were stories, told by those who had ventured to the temple in search of peace, that Barbarik's presence could still be felt. They spoke of a gentle wind that whispered through the trees, a quiet voice that urged them to look beyond the world's illusions, to seek the truth that lay hidden beneath the surface.

And among those who came to the temple was a young man an heir to the throne of Hastinapura. He was a child of the Pandavas' bloodline, but his heart was troubled by the same questions that had once haunted Barbarik. The young prince, no longer content with the glittering promises of kingship, had heard the whispers of Barbarik's name in the halls of the palace, in the gardens of the old temple, and in the stories passed down through generations.

One day, as he stood at the altar of the temple, staring at the stone inscriptions, the prince felt a strange, unexplainable presence behind him. It was as though the very air had shifted, as though the winds themselves carried with them the weight of a thousand unspoken words. He closed his eyes and listened.

The voice that spoke to him was not loud, nor was it forceful. It was a whisper gentle and persistent carrying with it the weight of a warrior's sacrifice.

"Victory is not measured by the battles won, nor by the throne you claim," the voice said. "True victory lies in the peace you bring to others, the wisdom you impart, and the legacy you leave in the hearts of those who follow you."

The prince stood there for what seemed like hours, the weight of the voice settling deep within him. When he opened his eyes, the temple was empty, but he felt a shift within his own soul a sense of understanding, of clarity that had long eluded him.

It was then that he knew the truth of Barbarik's sacrifice, the purpose of his offering. Barbarik had not given his head for victory, nor for glory. He had given it for a future, for a world that would learn from the mistakes of its past. He had given it as a reminder that power and strength were not the measures of greatness, but rather the ability to live in truth, to carry one's burdens without bitterness, and to offer peace to a broken world.

As the young prince left the temple that day, he felt a new resolve rise within him. He would be a ruler not for the power he could wield, but for the legacy of peace he could build. And in the years to come, when he sat upon the throne of Hastinapura, he would always remember the whispers of Barbarik, the warrior who had no body but whose soul had shaped the very fabric of history.

And so, Barbarik's legend lived on not as a tale of war, but as a story of sacrifice, wisdom, and redemption. His head, still resting in the stone temple, watched over the world in silence. His journey, though cut short in the mortal realm, had never truly ended. For as long as the wind still whispered through the trees of Kurukshetra, Barbarik remained. He was the eternal witness to the world's pain, its growth, and its triumphs.

www.ingramcontent.com/pod-product-compliance
Lightning Source LLC
Chambersburg PA
CBHW022229160726
47991CB00016B/2666